Philippe Claudel

DOG ISLAND

Translated from the French by
Euan Cameron

MACLEHOSE PRESS
QUERCUS · LONDON

First published as *L'Archipel du Chien*
by Editions Stock, Paris, in 2018
First published in Great Britain in 2020 by MacLehose Press
This paperback edition published in 2021 by

MacLehose Press
An imprint of Quercus Publishing Ltd
Carmelite House
50 Victoria Embankment
London EC4Y 0DZ
An Hachette UK company

Co-funded by the
Creative Europe Programme
of the European Union

This publication has been funded with support from the European Commission. This publication reflects the views only of the author, and the Commission cannot be held responsible for any use which may be made of the information contained within.

A CIP catalogue record for this book is available from the British Library.

ISBN (MMP) 978 1 52940 065 6
ISBN (Ebook) 978 1 52940 063 2

Designed and typeset in Quadraat by Libanus Press Ltd
Printed and bound in Great Britain by Clays Ltd, Elcograf S.p.A.

MIX
Paper from responsible sources
FSC® C104740
www.fsc.org

Papers used by MacLehose Press are from well-managed forests and other responsible sources.

Let me know at what time I shall be carried on board.

LAST WORDS WRITTEN BY ARTHUR RIMBAUD

Be happy if you are allowed to breathe again after grieving
And blessed if death relieves you of all sorrow.

GIACOMO LEOPARDI

I

YOU LUST AFTER GOLD AND SCATTER ASHES.

You tarnish beauty, destroy innocence.

You allow great streams of mud to flow everywhere. Hatred is your nourishment, indifference your compass. You are creatures of slumber, forever sleeping, even when you think you are awake. You are the fruit of a listless age. Your anxieties are ephemeral, butterflies that are quickly hatched, and immediately charred by the light of day. Your hands mould your life into a drab, dry clay. You are consumed by your loneliness. Your selfishness makes you flabby. You turn your backs on your brothers and you surrender your souls. Your natures fester on neglect.

How will future centuries judge your generation?

The story we are about to discover is as real as you may be. It takes place here, just as it could have happened there. It would be too easy to think that it happened elsewhere. The names of the people who live in this place matter little. We could change them. Put your own names in their place. You are so alike, products of the same immutable mould.

I am sure that sooner or later you will ask a legitimate

question: have you really witnessed what you are telling us? I reply: yes, I did witness it. Just as you did, although you did not wish to look. You never want to look. I am the one who reminds you. I am the intruder. I see everything. I know everything. But I am nothing and I fully intend to remain so. Neither man nor woman. Quite simply, I am the voice. It is from the darkness that I shall tell you the story.

The events that I shall relate occurred yesterday. A few days ago. A year or two ago. Not more. I say "yesterday" but it seems to me that I ought to say "today". Mankind does not like yesterday. People live in the present and dream of the days to come.

The story takes place on an island. An ordinary island. Neither large nor small. Not very far from the country upon which it is dependent, but which has forgotten all about it, and close to a different continent to the one it belongs to, but of which it takes no notice.

One of the Dog Islands.

When you search for this archipelago on the maps, you do not notice the Dog at first glance. It is hidden. The children have trouble finding it. The teacher whom they have already nicknamed the Old Woman was amused by their efforts, then by their surprise when, with the tip of her ruler, she sketched the outlines of its jaw. The Dog suddenly emerged. They were frightened by it. It was like being with certain people whose character you do not really know when you first spend time with them, who one day bite off your head.

The Dog is there, drawn on the flimsy paper. Mouth open, teeth bared. Ready to tear to pieces a long, pale patch of cobalt blue which the map has sprinkled with figures indicating the depths and some arrows that show the tides. Its jaws are two curved islands, its tongue also forms an island, and so do its teeth, some of them pointed, others massive and square-shaped, others again tapered like daggers. Its teeth, therefore, are islands. Among them is the one where this story takes place, the only inhabited one, at the very end of the lower jaw. Right beside the vast blue prey that does not know that it is coveted.

Life on the island derives from the volcano that dominates it and which for thousands of years has spewed out its lava and its fertile scoria. It is known as the Brau. The name has a barbaric ring. It used to frighten the little ones, once upon a time, when the island delighted to the cries and laughter of children. Nowadays, after its last angry outburst, the Brau is digesting. Its crater is usually shrouded in a blanket of mist. It is allowing itself a very long siesta. A few rumbles from time to time. Muffled noises. The restless tremors of a slumberer, who shudders and goes back to sleep.

The rest of the skeleton of the Dog is a mass of tiny islets, the majority of them minute, like crumbs of bread left on the tablecloth at the end of a meal. Deserted. By contrast, the one we are about to discover has pounded to the throbbing of men's blood. It lingers there, like a piece of the world that has fallen into the azure sea. In its earliest days, there would probably have been a population of fishermen, in the time of the Phoenicians, descendants of pirates and thieves whose boats had run aground there, or who had hidden ashore to count their spoils.

There are vines, olive groves, caper orchards. Each cultivated acre bears witness to the stubbornness of those ancestors who patiently snatched it from the volcano. On this island you are either a farmer or a fisherman. There are no other choices. Young people frequently want neither the one nor the other. They leave. The departures are never followed by homecomings. That is how it is and always has been.

The Dog spews out inhumane seasons. Summer dries up the people and strikes them down. Winter chills them to the bone. Bitter wind and cold rain. Months of shivering lethargy. Their houses have been around the world. In photographs. In magazines. Without even asking, architects, ethnologists and historians have decided that they belong to the heritage of mankind. This made the islanders laugh, before it irritated them. They can neither destroy the houses nor convert them.

Those who do not live there envy them. The idiots. Built of badly pointed lava brick, the houses look like huge huts built by a population of dwarves. They are harsh to live in. Uncomfortable. Dark and rough. You either suffocate or you freeze in them. They surround the islanders and they oppress them. Eventually the islanders come to resemble them.

The island's wine is a sweet and heavy red that derives from a variety of grape which grows only here, the marula. The buds of the grapes look like magpies' eyes: small, black, shiny, and without any bloom. Harvested in about mid-September, the grapes are then laid on the walls of the vineyards and caper orchards, protected from birds by thin nets. They dry there for two weeks before being pressed, then the juice is left to ferment in the darkness of long, narrow cellars that are hewn from the slopes of the Brau.

When the wine is bottled later, it has taken on the colour of bull's blood. You cannot see the light through it. It is a child of the depths and the belly of the earth. It is the wine of the Gods. When you dip your lips into it, it is sunshine and honey that come into your mouth and flow down your throat, as well as the bottomless chasm of the other side of the world. Old people used to say as they drank it that they were simultaneously sucking at the breasts of Aphrodite and of Hades.

II

IT WAS A MONDAY MORNING IN SEPTEMBER, ON THE beach, when it all began. It is called the beach, for want of a better term, even though nobody can swim there on account of the reefs and the tide, nor relax on it because it is made up of rough, sharp volcanic shingle.

The Old Woman walked there every day. The Old Woman was the former teacher. Everyone on the island had passed through her class. She knows all the families. She was born here and she will die here. No-one has ever seen her smile. They scarcely know her age. Probably not very far off eighty. Five years previously, she had been obliged to give up the class. From then on she took her daily walk early in the morning, with her dog, a mongrel with melancholy eyes, who liked nothing so much as chasing after the seagulls.

She was always alone on the beach. Whatever the weather, nothing in the world would make her give up this walk by the sea, in this desolate place which you would think had been snatched from a northern country, from Scandinavia or Iceland, and tossed down there just to irritate people.

That morning, the dog was prancing around her as it usually did, leaping up at the taunting large birds. It had begun to rain. Still only a light, cold drizzle, and the sea was rolling in with mean waves, short and strained, that broke upon the shore in a dirty foam.

The dog stopped all of a sudden, barked, and set off on a mad run that took it fifty metres or so away, towards three long shapes that the swell of the tide had thrown up on the beach, but which it was still tossing around, as though reluctant to relinquish them completely. The dog caught their scent, turned towards the Old Woman and let out a long howl.

At that moment, two men also noticed the shapes on the beach: America, a bachelor who produced a little wine and was something of an odd-job man, who from time to time came to inspect what the tide had thrown up, cans that had fallen overboard, lost wooden planks, nets, ropes, bits of floating wood. He saw the strange shapes in the distance, got down from his cart, patted the flank of his donkey, and told it not to move, to stay there, on the path. There was also Swordy, so called because, although he was not very bright, he was without question one of the best catchers of swordfish on the island, knowing the habits of the great fish – the depths at which it lay, its moods and cycles – and able to fathom its routes and tricks.

The boats had not gone out that day. The weather was too bad. Swordy worked for the Mayor, who was the biggest fishing employer on the island. He owned three motor boats and cold storage rooms in which to keep his fish, along with those of ten other skippers who were too poor to possess their own.

Two days earlier, while everyone was away at sea, a gust of wind had blown away three buoys with some lobster pots that

Swordy had set down in the open sea, having borrowed the boat for a full day and a night, with the agreement of the Mayor.

That Monday morning, he had come to the beach to see whether the tide might have brought them in. It was the dog's long howl that alerted him. He was walking at some distance from the Old Woman, who had not heard him. He saw her accelerate suddenly and stumble on the shingle, almost fall, and recover herself. He sensed that something was wrong.

He spotted America, who had just left his cart and was also walking towards the dog.

All three – the Old Woman, Swordy and America – arrived at the same time at the spot where the drenched shapes were bobbing about in the waves. The dog looked at its mistress, let out another little bark, then sniffed at what the sea had just produced: the bodies of three black men, simply dressed in T-shirts and jeans, barefooted, apparently sleeping, their faces against the shore.

The Old Woman spoke first, "What are you waiting for? Pull them out!"

The two men looked at one another and then did as the Old Woman said. They were not sure how to pick up the corpses and hesitated. They eventually took them by the arms and dragged them out backwards, laying them side by side on the dark shingle.

"You can't leave them like that! Turn them over."

Again, they hesitated, but eventually they managed to tip the bodies on their sides and suddenly the faces of the dead men appeared.

They were less than twenty years of age. Their eyes were closed. They seemed to have dropped into a harsh sleep that had twisted their lips and marbled their skin with great patches of violet, lending their faces an impenetrable expression that resembled a reproach.

The Old Woman, America and Swordy all made the sign of the cross at the same time. The dog barked, three times. The voice of the Old Woman was heard once more:

"America, do you have a tarpaulin in your cart?"

America nodded. He walked away.

"You, Swordy, go and warn the Mayor. Don't talk to anyone else. Come back with him. Don't delay."

Swordy did not argue and he set off at a run. Death had always frightened him. You could hear the sea after the gust of wind that had swept over the island during the night, and you could even smell it inside the houses because it had cast its salty spittle beneath the doors, between the disjointed stones and down the chimneys. He had slept badly too, tossing and turning in bed, getting up to pee or drink a glass of water.

The Old Woman and the dog stayed near the corpses. They looked like a painting in a museum – instructive, but it made you wonder what moral it could be illustrating: the infinity of the sea, the bodies of three young black men, an old woman and a dog standing beside them. You sensed that it must mean something, but could not have said what it was.

America returned with a blue plastic tarpaulin.

"Cover them," the Old Woman said.

The bodies disappeared beneath the synthetic shroud. America placed some large pebbles along the edges to stop the wind blowing it away, but it still managed to sweep through underneath. This made a tearing, ruffling sound, like the big top of a circus.

"Where do you think they come from, Miss?"

In spite of his forty years, his large manly fingers, and his face that was as chapped as an old bar of soap, America found his anxiety and his childish voice returning. He lit a cigarette.

"Where do you think?" said the Old Woman abruptly.

America shrugged and took a puff, waiting for a truth he dared not utter to be mentioned. But when the Old Woman said nothing, he murmured, hesitating like a pupil unsure of his response, and jutting his chin in the direction of the pale distance to the south.

"From over there . . . ?"

"Of course from over there! They didn't fall from the sky! You were never very smart but you watch television like everyone else, don't you?"

III

Swordy had not delayed. Less than half an hour later, they saw him coming back, rounding the tall rock that blocked the beach and concealed it from the view of the town and the port. The Mayor was following, but there was also another figure, large and cumbersome, that of the Doctor.

The Old Woman cursed under her breath when she spotted him. The dog welcomed the new arrivals by seeking pats it did not receive.

"So what's all the mystery about, this idiot wouldn't tell me a thing!"

Swordy hung his head. The Mayor was irritable. He was as thin as an anchovy, with a lean, sallow face and grey hair. He was sixty. The same age as the Doctor, whom he had known since childhood, but the latter was the size and shape of a barrel, bald and ruddy. A large moustache, dyed black, covered his upper lip. He was struggling to regain his breath, dressed in a linen suit that had once been elegant, but which was now covered in stains and had holes in various places. The Mayor was wearing fisherman's overalls.

"I told Swordy to tell only you."

"The Doctor and I were still working on that damn plan for the Thermal Baths! Are you going to tell us what's going on, at some point?"

"Show them."

America understood. He bent down and removed three of the stones keeping the tarpaulin in place. The wind flew into it and created the shape of a plump belly. At the same moment, two large, alarming seagulls dropped from the sky. They skimmed over the men, who instinctively drew their heads into their shoulders, before the birds rose up again and vanished into the clouds.

At the sight of the bodies, the Doctor dropped his convenient smile for a brief second. The Mayor cursed, using the old dialect, in which Arabic has mingled with Spanish and Greek for a thousand years and more. He frowned, and his forehead became heavily wrinkled, an indication of the circumstances he could see arising from this discovery, and of which he was swiftly taking stock.

But the strangest thing, and frankly the most unreal, was that a new voice rose up, one that did not belong to any of those present; a voice that caused them all to jump, as though the Devil had suddenly decided to join them.

In the confusion of their thoughts and the growing awareness that the sight before them did not belong to a nightmare, a scene from a film or a television newsreel, or a page from a crime novel, but to the damp reality of this September morning, they had not heard the approach of the newcomer who had just broken the silence, like a lanced boil, by simply repeating "My God!" three times over, in a soft and horrified voice that made them all shudder, and immediately irritated them all, since no-one likes to be caught in flagrante by weakness and fear.

The voice belonged to the Teacher, who had taken over the class after the Old Woman. He was not native to the island. A foreigner. The Old Woman did not like him, but then she did not like many people. Of course, it had been some time since she had stepped down, but she still thought of him as a thief. He had stolen her job. Stolen her pupils. Stolen her school. She loathed him.

He had a wife who was said to be a nurse. To begin with, she had looked for work, but nothing had been offered to her. She had then tried to open a health care clinic in an annexe of the school. But the people of the island look after themselves and when it is something more serious there is the Doctor. So in the end she had remained at home. Doing nothing, apart from finding that time passed very slowly. The island had become her tedious day-to-day chore.

People said that she was wasting away like a forgotten plant on the corner of a windowsill, one that is hardly ever watered. The couple had two little girls, twins. Gay and carefree as young birds. Two ten-year-old children, who never left one another's side and only played with each other.

That morning, the Teacher was dressed in green shorts and a close-fitting white T-shirt, on which was printed the advertising slogan for a telephone company. He was wearing trainers. He shaved his calves and his thighs like a professional sportsman, his skin was smooth like a woman's. Every morning, he set off on a long training run before taking a shower and going to work. His attention was gripped solely by the three corpses, whereas everyone else was now staring only at him.

"What on earth are you doing here?" the Mayor barked.

"I was running. I saw the cart and America's donkey. And all of you in the distance. And then the tarpaulin. I reckoned that—"

"What did you reckon?"

The Old Woman had spoken in as unpleasant a tone of voice as the Mayor.

"That all this was not normal – that something serious must have happened. I recognised the Doctor, and then the Mayor . . . My God!"

He did not disguise the fact that he was deeply distressed, unlike the others, who were also upset but would have died rather than let it show. In spite of his large, sturdy body, and the strength that radiated from his youth, for he was a little over thirty years old, he suddenly looked very vulnerable. He was unable to stop the flow of his litany in which the name of God trickled like clear water.

The Old Woman stopped the tap for him.

"Leave God out of all this."

The Teacher fell silent. No-one spoke.

It was early. Only just eight o'clock. The cloud covering had dropped still lower, and the dawning day was already losing its brightness. The wind from the sea blew the waves right up to the feet of the little group, who all took a few steps backwards so as not to get wet. Everyone suddenly felt cold. The Teacher was shivering, the flesh on his arms and his legs looked like a plucked chicken's. Only the three corpses remained impassive.

The Mayor spoke.

"There are six of us here. Six of us who know. Six who should say nothing until this evening, when we shall meet again at the town hall at nine o'clock. I am going to think about what steps to take."

"Steps to take?" said the Teacher in surprise, shivering.

"Be quiet!" the Mayor said. "We'll discuss the matter this evening. But if between now and then one of you talks to anyone about this, or if any one of you does not turn up this evening, I'll take down my gun and I'll sort him out."

"What are you going to do with them?" asked the Old Woman gesturing to the three corpses.

"Swordy and I will take care of them. America, leave us your cart and your donkey. The rest of you, you can all leave. You too, America, two of us will be enough. See you this evening. And remember, I'm not a man to make empty promises!"

They all dispersed. The Old Woman continued her walk as though nothing had happened. The dog gambolled around her. It was as happy as only animals can be, who live in the present, who know nothing about the past, nor about suffering and matters concerning the future.

The Old Woman disappeared into the distance. The Teacher tried to resume his route, but he could be seen lurching and eventually walking aimlessly, like a robot, turning back to gaze at the corpses of the drowned men. The Doctor set off towards the town with America, while Swordy returned with the donkey and the cart. The Mayor rummaged in his pockets.

"Are you looking for something, Boss?"

"A cigarette."

"I thought you had given up."

"And if I want to start again, is it anything to do with you?"

"I was just asking."

"Give me one of yours."

Swordy held out a pack. The Mayor helped himself to a cigarette and Swordy lit it for him. The Mayor took two long drags one after the other, closing his eyes. Swordy stroked the donkey as he contemplated the three bodies.

"And now, Boss?"

"'Now' what?"

"What's going to happen?"

The Mayor shrugged. He spat on the ground.

"Nothing. Nothing is going to happen. It was an error."

"An error?"

"In a few weeks' time you'll tell yourself you dreamed all this. And if you speak to me about it, if you ask me anything, I'll tell you I don't know what you're talking about. Do you understand?"

"I don't know."

"Memories. We can hold on to them, but we can also grate them up like a piece of cheese in the soup. And afterwards, they no longer exist. Do you understand that?"

"That I understand. The cheese disappears. It melts into the soup. All that's left is the taste in the mouth, but with a glass of wine you get rid of it. Nothing is left."

"There you are. With a glass of wine, you get rid of it. Let's go, the Old Woman is staring at us."

The Old Woman had stopped some hundred metres away and even appeared to be turning back, as though she were coming towards them with her dagger-shaped figure and her dog that pranced around her. Swordy grabbed the first corpse under the armpits. The Mayor took it by the feet. They hoisted it onto the cart, and did the same with the two others. Swordy lay the tarpaulin over them and tied it down. Soon, all one could see was blue plastic. The Mayor had already clambered up onto the plank that served as a seat. Swordy joined him, took the reins, made the donkey turn around and set it off in the direction of the path.

The beach returned to its impassive solitude.

IV

FOR EACH OF THESE CHARACTERS, THE DAY HAD FELT AS long as a century and it was with relief that they watched dusk fall. At nine o'clock that evening, while the night outside blurred the sea and the sky into one dark mass, the Mayor shut the door of the boardroom and drew the velvet curtains that were never closed. Clouds of red dust dispersed and scattered over the two chandeliers, the only luxury in the room, and landed on the heads and shoulders of those who had taken their places around the oval table.

The Mayor sat down. He did so with ostentatious solemnity, his small body like that of an elderly child, and, in silence still, looked at each of those present: no-one who had been on the beach that morning was missing.

"Swordy and I have placed the remains in a place where no-one will be able to find them, and to which I alone have the key."

He took out of his pocket a piece of aluminium that did not look like a conventional key, something flat and smooth, dotted with holes, and placed it in front of him. He gave the others time to look at it.

"I've spent the day considering what should be done, and I suppose you have been doing so too."

The Teacher, who had changed his sporting gear for appropriate clothes and whose demeanour still showed evidence of the great anxiety that exercised him, interrupted the Mayor:

"How do you mean, 'what should be done'? We must inform the authorities! What else? I was so flabbergasted this morning that I wasn't in my right mind. I did as you asked, I haven't said anything to anyone, but I don't understand what we are doing here or why you are delaying getting in touch with the police and a magistrate. To allow an entire day to go by, after such a discovery – it's astonishing!"

The Teacher stopped speaking. Looking at the others, he searched for support, but they lowered their heads, apart from the Doctor, who smiled as he gazed at him, and the Old Woman, whose bright eyes caused him to look away. He was breathing quickly, and swallowing with difficulty. The Mayor stared at him for a moment before replying:

"I remind you that my role as mayor places police matters within my remit on this island, and that in the absence of a police station I am the only person among the inhabitants to have this power, a power that I have never used, as you are no doubt aware, because ours is a peaceful island. And although I have no skills where matters of justice are concerned, it nonetheless falls to me to decide initially whether it is worthwhile involving an investigator and a magistrate from the mainland."

"And three corpses, are they not worthwhile?" said the Teacher. "How many would it require for you to pick up your telephone? Five, ten, twenty, a hundred?"

His audacity made him blush. He stared once more at the

Mayor, whose eyes appeared to be bulging in their sockets and who could be heard grinding his teeth. The latter retorted, in a voice so low that some of them had to strain their ears to hear him.

"The bodies have been examined by the Doctor. They display no traces of violence. Stop me if I am mistaken: you didn't notice any wounds, isn't that what you told me?"

The Doctor, who was rubbing his stomach, assented with a smile.

"Nothing indicates that these unfortunate people were the victims of an attack or murder. They died by drowning and did not spend long in the water, as is indicated by the lack of abrasions, or of wounds that might have been caused by rocks, crabs or fish, or the propellers of a boat—"

"Did you carry out an autopsy on them, Doctor?" the Teacher said, and on asking this question he swallowed painfully, as though the word, heard thousands of times on detective series, was too burdensome for him.

"No need," replied the Doctor, maintaining his good humour. "Drowning, alas, is obvious. What did you expect they died from? Sunstroke?"

Swordy laughed, and so did America. Even the Old Woman smiled, silently, her pale lips curled into a haughty pout over her grey teeth. And the Mayor laughed too, but in his case it sounded like the hiss of a snake. The Teacher, who was wriggling about on his chair, spoke out in his timid little boy's voice, which did not correspond to his large, strong frame.

"You know better than I do that, to establish whether someone has died from drowning, a superficial examination is insufficient, and that comparative analyses of the levels of strontium and iron in the blood and the levels of these metals in the water are vital. I apologise for these somewhat technical details. I don't mean to play the pedant; I am simply interested in the truth."

"It's entirely to your credit," replied the Doctor, who had begun to fondle a cigar that he had just taken from his inside coat pocket, "and you are right. But let us consider for a minute: everyone here knows where these unfortunate people come from, and what they were attempting to do. Even if we turn our backs on it, Africa is right there, very close, a few dozen kilometres away. How can we not know what is taking place there, when the media never stop showing us the lengths that thousands of wretched people go to in order to reach Europe? We know very well where these three men wanted to go. The boat in which they had set out capsized, as did others before it, and as others will capsize again. They died from drowning. The sea often allows men to glide over its surface, but occasionally it grows irritable and devours some of them. That is the truth, which is extremely sad, I grant you."

Talking had made the Doctor feel hot and he took out a handkerchief to mop the drops of sweat that had appeared on his brow. The Teacher said nothing, it was as though the Doctor's speech had acted on him like a narcotic. The Mayor let him wallow in his silence. The Old Woman continued to glare at him. Swordy stared at the ceiling and America solemnly inspected his fingernails, as if their blackness suddenly bothered him greatly, and had plunged him into depths of astonishment.

It was then that a sort of scraping could be heard at the door, not timid knocking, but an unpleasant noise, like a branch of dead wood scraping against a shutter in the wind, or when a crow tries to get into a house with its beak and its claws. And even before any of them had been able to identify the sound, the door slowly opened – one might have thought that it was the wind beating against the casement again. The Priest appeared, with his thick spectacles and his neck as hairless as an anaemic cockerel's, strangled by the loose collar of his cassock that had once been white, but which time and dirt had turned as grey as a hangman's rope. A few bees buzzed around him.

The Mayor did not permit him to come in any further.

"Father, please forgive us, but we are busy with an important meeting and I don't—"

"Don't worry," the Priest said. "I know why you are here. The bodies of the black men on the beach this morning. I've been told everything."

"Which of these bastards told you?" the Mayor shouted. He had leaped out of his seat, beating the tabletop with both hands. He looked at everybody as though he was about to throttle them.

"Somebody confided to me in the secrecy of the confessional," the Priest continued. "That person is here present. They should not be afraid, I would never betray them. I simply warned them that I would be coming this evening. My presence is no surprise to them. I simply wanted you to be aware, all and every one of you, that I know. My place is here, therefore, with you."

He always gave the impression of being at home everywhere, even in places where he had never set foot. He removed his thick and cloudy spectacles, which made him look like a goldfish lost in an aquarium where the algae had turned the glass green, then began to polish them slowly with a strip of his soutane, which smelled of camphor and lengthy celibacy.

"Do go on, please. Where were you?" he asked, once he had wiped his spectacles again and knocked a bee that would not stop buzzing around his ear to the ground.

The Mayor clenched his jaw. He fiddled with his propelling pencil. His skin looked as though it had grown tauter still over the bones of his face. He was most likely trying to reason with himself, telling himself that a priest was not really a man, and that, through holding long conversations in empty space, he had, in his deep solitude and wretchedness, lost his sense of reality and was out of touch with the world. He was probably only there to concern himself with what was to become of the souls of the drowned men, and if that were the case, he as mayor and out-and-out atheist would gladly allow him to fulfil his purpose. He could not care less about the salvation of souls, Purgatory, Hell and all that nonsense. His training as an accountant by correspondence course had long ago taught him that life was merely an earthly sum of joyful and unhappy moments which, ultimately, whatever one did, amounted to a nil balance sheet.

Nevertheless, the Priest's words had their effect. Around the table, people gave one another suspicious looks. Each of them tried to guess who it could have been who hurried along to the church, still believing sufficiently in those questions of confession and forgiveness to have felt the need to knock at the door of the presbytery and then to shut themselves inside a dusty old cupboard in order to soothe their soul.

What was certain was that the man or woman who had gone to tell the Priest everything was covering it up very well, because each one of them had appeared to be horrified when he announced that he knew everything. But in reality, it was a strange, exaggerated type of horror, because up until now no-one had been guilty of any crime. No-one had drowned the three men. No-one had thrown them in the water. No-one knew them or had met them before.

The meeting had to continue. The appearance of the Priest seemed to calm the Teacher. Perhaps he thought that the Priest would side with him and ask, as he did, for the authorities to be informed immediately. So he allowed the Mayor to speak, without interrupting him this time.

"As the Doctor has mentioned, we know very well where these men come from. They are fleeing poverty. They are fleeing chaos. They are fleeing war. They are risking their lives by setting out on rafts, dinghies and wrecks that can sink at any moment. The Doctor has confirmed: they are not the first to die like this. They will not, alas, be the last. What is new is that the tides should have brought them to our shore. It's hard to understand."

The Mayor paused for a second, time enough for him to glance at the Teacher, thinking that he was about to break into this silence, but the latter did nothing and waited to hear what followed.

"Our island was not their destination," the Mayor went on. "They probably did not even know it existed. It has become their cemetery. If I were to inform the police and a magistrate, what would happen? Not only would we see those fine gentlemen, who always look down on us as though we were rats' droppings, but they would be followed by masses of reporters, with their microphones and their cameras. From one day to the next, our island would become the isle of the drowned. You know how keen those vultures are on such phrases."

The Mayor continued:

"If the press suddenly gets hold of this and paints an appalling picture of our island, how, in such circumstances, can we complete our Thermal Baths project with the Consortium? Do you think they would still be willing to invest millions and build their complex? Our land, which is famous for its hot water springs, its landscapes, its wine, its oil and its capers, would it not become one where corpses from Africa get washed up? Our pure waters, would they not become those where dead bodies soak, stew and rot? Who would then want to swim, take water cures, or eat the fish that are caught there?"

The Mayor paused for a moment, allowing the words he had just spoken to sink into the mind of each one of them and unfurl their gruesome images.

"I am the Mayor," he went on. "I am responsible for the present and I must also think of the future of our island, and of our children, most of whom are forced to leave because there is too little work here. The Thermal Baths project will create jobs. A hundred or so when fully operational. Not counting all the people required for its construction. I don't want to wreck this project. It's our opportunity. Our last opportunity for families to remain here, and their children, and their children's children. Nothing, alas, will revive these three poor wretches. Letting the public know what has happened risks dreadful consequences and it will not bring them back to life. Don't take umbrage at my comments, Father. Naturally, I don't have the authority to tell you how to behave, but I do appeal to everyone's good sense, to your responsibility and to your fellow feeling."

There was a long, dazed silence, filled with awkwardness. Some of them probably thought that the Teacher, who was wriggling about in his chair, would speak out again and question what the Mayor had just said, but he did nothing and merely scratched his woolly blond hair nervously.

The Priest was silent. He was rocking on his chair and had folded his hands over his stomach, which, over the years, had assumed the shape of a thrush's egg, pointed yet bulging.

"Where did you put them?"

The voice of the Old Woman broke the silence like a glass smashing on a tile.

"In a safe place, I've already said."

"I'm not asking you whether the place is safe, I'm asking you where it is."

"What difference would it make for you to know?"

"You want our silence? I want the truth. That's all."

The Mayor tried to hold the Old Woman's gaze but he lost himself in her milky eyes. Irritated by his own weakness, he looked away. Then he noticed that the others were all staring at him, without exception, waiting for him to reply.

"In my cold room," he eventually said, in a low voice.

"In your cold room? With the fish?" said the Teacher, who seemed shocked and frightened at the same time.

"Where would you expect me to put them? In my bed?" And the Mayor, beside himself, broke the propelling pencil he was holding in his fingers without even realising he had done so.

V

IT WAS A CURIOUS PROCESSION WHICH, IN TOTAL silence, left the Mayor's office that evening shortly after ten o'clock. In single file, the Mayor at the head and the Priest bringing up the rear, it made its way – slipping through the darkness of the narrow streets – towards that area of the port where the fish market, the workshops in which boats are repaired, and the dry docks are situated, as well as the cold storage warehouse.

Set slightly apart from the other buildings and painted red and yellow, the warehouse has two entrances: the one facing the sea enables the Mayor's three boats to transfer their catch into a tiled room where it is sorted and packaged; and the other, on the quayside, gives access to the company's offices, to the shed where the fishermen store their equipment, change their clothes and repair their nets, and to the actual cold room.

The Mayor left it to Swordy to remove the padlock from the chain that kept the gate closed. It went five or six times around the gateposts, and when the fisherman took it off it produced a clanking, swishing, rusty music. It was as though he had just removed a convict's chains from his ankles. Swordy pushed open the gate and allowed the Mayor to pass.

The little group made its way inside. The Mayor pulled a bunch of keys out of his pocket, chose one without hesitating and fitted it into the lock of a gateway that was reinforced with plywood panels. He pushed with his shoulder against the door, which had been affected by the damp. The door opened. He pressed a switch and returned to the group, to whom he gave a signal, with a nervous twitch of his hand, that they should enter as quickly as possible. He shut the door behind the Priest with another shove of his shoulder.

Three high ceiling lights dispersed a harsh beam over the ropes and cables, the nets, the plastic and wooden crates, the buoys, the pots of paint and tar, the oilskins and the boots, the cork floats and all the usual clutter found in fishermen's storerooms.

Whiffs of salt, dried seaweed, oil, dog hair and tobacco, and fish too, mingled with all of this. In a corner, four chairs, placed around a chest upon which a collection of dirty, odd mugs had been left, seemed to be waiting for people to play cards or chat. Promotional calendars for brands of motors were pinned up in one corner. You could make out the days and months of years long past, and the photographs of naked young women that illustrated them had faded over time, giving their enormous breasts a waxy tint.

At the end of the huge room an aluminium door could be seen. It was tall, rounded and surprisingly new, and it made one think of the airlock in a spacecraft, like those in science fiction films. It was the door to the cold storage room. The Mayor was standing beside it.

"We're not going to spend the night here!"

They all felt as though they were in a museum and they looked around as though they were discovering a new world: the Doctor was walking about with his hands behind his back like a philosopher out for a stroll. The Priest was adjusting a lopsided crucifix that was wedged between two pornographic pictures he pretended not to notice. America, dazzled by the nylon mesh of a brand-new net, was stroking it lovingly, but abandoned it for some cans of asphalt which were spilling their syrupy contents on the ground in long, thin streaks resembling witch's hair. Swordy was looking for something, in an oilskin that must have belonged to him. The Old Woman, who had positioned herself right in the middle of the warehouse, was swivelling on her feet, slowly inspecting the entire space 360 degrees around her. She could have been mistaken for a bailiff assessing the value of each object before putting it up for auction. As for the Teacher, he was carefully studying a marine chart placed under glass on which the island could be seen, as well as the other isles in the Dog Islands. Faint arrows marked the principal currents. The shallow areas were coloured grey and the reefs violet.

The voice of the Mayor shook them out of their daydreams and everyone turned towards him. He had inserted the strange key he had produced a little earlier in the evening into the lock. Once the mechanism was unblocked, he made two attempts to open the door, which eventually gave way with a rubber-like noise, similar to the one made when you unblock a drain with a plunger.

A polar blast suddenly froze their faces as a mist of icy vapours enveloped them, giving them the sense that they were entering another season, far away from their world, from their quiet, warm existence, far from life. They all shivered at the same moment, due to the temperature which was kept at two degrees in the first part of the room, but also because the vision of perforated crates, in which the previous day's catch had been put, suddenly revealed a rigid stack of silvery, iridescent creatures with their mouths wide open and their eyes wreathed in grey and green reflections.

Most of the crates contained sea bass, small bonitos, rockfish, mullets, rainbow wrasse, octopuses and scabbardfish, and all the usual mass from the depths that the nets had dragged up and which the fishermen had then placed on beds of ice.

Hanging from the ceiling by hooks to which their tail fins had been tied, two large swordfish and a tuna looked as though they were suffering agonies. The "swords" of the former were dragging, uselessly, on the ground and their big eyes were begging for release. As for the tuna, an enormous one, it resembled a plump landsknecht caparisoned in his armour, fallen in a battle that had left him with no obvious wound. Resigned, he was staring at the ground as if to discover the reasons for his defeat there.

They had to pass close to these large hanging creatures in order to follow the Mayor into the second part of the cold storage room which, behind another aluminium door, housed the freezer. Again, once the door was opened, vapours escaped that were icier still than the previous ones, and they eventually caused the small group to freeze. The Doctor's smile now looked like a grimace and his moustache, together with the frizzy eyebrows of the Teacher, were quickly covered with what resembled artificial snow. Everybody shivered, with the notable exception of the Old Woman, even though she was only dressed in a thin woollen cardigan.

The freezer room was dark. The vapours that emanated from it only succeeded in edging the darkness with a cloudy, shifting greyness that no-one managed to identify. The Mayor left them puzzling over everything for a few seconds, for he was anxious to create a dramatic effect. Then he pulled a lever which produced a dry banging sound, and a surgical light immediately lit up the entire space, obliging the little group to close their eyes for a brief moment as though they had been pushed, in a playful gesture, beneath the blinding spotlights of a television set.

The room was about eight metres square. On three of its walls partitions had been erected to store the fish. The one attached to the furthest wall was empty. Only a crust of ice, thick, uneven and denticulated, created a miniature ice shelf that was wrapped around its pedestal and from which stalactites drooped in two places, syrup-like, making them look like a large cat's canine teeth.

Cut up into slices, the head and upper body of a tuna lay in silvery discs on the right-hand partition. The fish's head, intact and arrogant-looking, still retained, solidly attached to it, a segment of about twenty centimetres of compact, reddish flesh which the cold had made iridescent with pale crystals, but which the saw had not damaged.

On the partition opposite, America's blue tarpaulin could be seen. The polar cold had accentuated its cracks and absurd corners. Shafts of vapour were escaping from the bundle.

The bodies twisted up inside the plastic shroud took up the entire storage space. Stiffened by the cold, the tarpaulin that covered their legs and their feet created a shape reminiscent of the sarcophagi of Ancient Egypt, but at the top, misshaped by the freezing cold, it had slipped down, allowing the face of one of the men to appear, gazing at the visitors. His eyelids were open, no doubt due to the cold. His eyes possessed neither irises nor pupils: bulging, they had become two white opaque glass balls.

The Priest, who had taken off his thick, bottle-dregs spectacles that had been frosted over by the icy vapour, wished to make this lifeless, inhuman expression disappear, and before the Mayor could prevent him he tried to close the dead eyelids, not realising that his gesture was pointless, since the wretched man's flesh had now acquired the hardness of marble.

And what the Priest had not thought about, either, was that the skin of his fingers would instantly stick to the large white eyes, the cold acting as the most effective of glues, and so he found that the pads of his right thumb and right index finger adhered to the pale eyeballs.

He let out a little moan of fear and surprise and tried to withdraw his hand, but two of his fingers remained attached to the dead man's eyes. Panic prevented him hearing the words of the Mayor, who was shouting and ordering him not to do anything and not to move, and asking Swordy to go and fetch a jug of hot water, quickly: with a brisk tug of his arm and a cry of pain, the Priest snatched his fingers away from the corpse.

Something that appeared unreal and fantastical to everyone then occurred: a dead man's face, black verging on grey, covered in frizzy hairs that were white with frost, whose eyes suddenly began to weep tears of blood which the cold immediately froze into tiny scarlet pearls.

VI

ON THE ISLAND, THE DEAD ARE BURIED STANDING UP. Earth is scarce. It is the most precious commodity. People had realised very quickly that it should belong to the living, that it was there to feed them, and that the dead should take up as little space as possible. That it was of no further use to them.

The town's cemetery therefore bristled with black stones, uneven in shape, barely a metre high, huddled together like the terrified soldiers of a devastated army, and upon which were carved the name of the deceased, the date of his or her birth and that of their death.

On the island, people live together, but in death they travel alone; the cemetery does not contain any communal or family graves, merely single tombs in which the dead person stands upright just as he or she stood upright in life.

The deaths of the three young black men had not taken place on the island. The sea had cast them onto the shore as though they were driftwood. No-one knew them and their previous lives had never crossed the lives of the island's inhabitants. Only their deaths had connected them, but that was not sufficient reason for the daily lives of those living there to be affected.

"Exaggerating a little," said the Mayor, once everyone had left the cold room and Swordy had applied bandages to the bleeding fingers of the Priest, who was screeching like a fledgling, "it is as though these three men have never existed, as though the tide has not brought their remains to us, as though – and this would have been most likely – the sea has carried them away and dissolved them in its depths as in an acid bath, and no-one knows what has become of them. If they had identity papers on them, it would be a different problem and a more difficult decision to take. Identity papers would have linked them to the world, to a country, a human administration, a history, a family. But here, there's nothing. Nothing to enable us to discover their names, their ages, the country from which they have fled. Nothing that can tell us whose sons, brothers, husbands or fathers they were."

"Holy shit, you're hurting me!" the Priest howled all of a sudden, which had the effect of interrupting the Mayor's comments and to arouse the three bees that were coming back to life on the shoulders of his cassock after the episode in the cold room.

"I'm doing what I can, Father," said Swordy. "I'm not a nurse."

"It's quite clear you're not the one who is in pain, either!"

The Doctor had refused with a smile to look after the Priest's fingers, offering the excuse that his own fingers were so awkward and podgy that he could not apply such small bandages. He had merely insisted that Swordy should disinfect the bare flesh, and so the fisherman had poured the remains of a bottle of marc on the wounds, which had already caused the Priest to cry out.

"You have understood my thoughts," the Mayor continued, "and you know very well that I am not a bastard, nor a man with no heart. But I'm not the one who created poverty in the world and it is not for me to mop it up on my own. To bury these three corpses in our cemetery makes no sense. For one thing, these men were not part of our community, but what's more, we don't even know what they believed in.

"In all probability they did not share our beliefs, and it would be insulting to put them in a place that has nothing to do with their religion. Furthermore, as I told you in the first place, I want this matter to be solely our concern and for us to keep it to ourselves, until we die without our having told anyone about it. Which, of course, requires that the corpses of these unfortunate men disappear, and for nothing to provide any further evidence of their presence anywhere."

The Mayor paused for a moment and scrutinised every face. Most of them bowed their heads, with the exception of the Old Woman, and the Teacher who, appalled, was staring at the Mayor and seemed to be gasping for air as though he were having an asthma attack.

"For a while, I thought it would be simplest to consign them to the sea. But how can we be sure that the sea will not wash up their bodies on our shore again? So I then said to myself that it would be best for us to bury them here, on our island, which is the last piece of land on which, without their being aware of it, they have come aground, the place where death has deposited them, delivering them from the suffering which has no doubt been their daily fate."

Swordy had finished bandaging up the Priest, but the Priest was not listening to the Mayor, and continued to grimace as he fiddled with his thick spectacles, as though by closely inspecting his fingers he would enable them to heal more quickly.

"I don't need to tell you that the island is pitted with chasms. Our ancestors thought these wells were the mouths of the Gods. I think there would be nothing sacrilegious or inhuman about our dropping the bodies of these three men into one of them. In a sense, they would be continuing their journey. They would reach the centre of the world and achieve eternal peace."

They all allowed the words of the Mayor to linger in their minds for a long time. As everyone feared, it was the Teacher who broke the silence:

"I'm dreaming! I must be dreaming! I feel as though I'm being rocked to sleep with a story! You speak too well, Mr Mayor! You want to get rid of the bodies of these poor men as though they were dust that one sweeps under a carpet! Do I have to remind you that certain filthy pigs on this island continue to empty their rubbish down those very same volcanic holes? Is that how you regard these wretched men's bodies, like rubbish? I should like to hear what Father has to say on this matter!"

When he realised that they were talking about him, the Priest looked up and stopped fiddling with his bandaged fingers, which he had been contemplating with a shattered expression. He was aware that everyone was looking at him and waiting for him to say something. He had probably heard the Mayor's comments and the brief exchange with the Teacher that followed, but it had been like music played in a distant room. He gave a long sigh, as if about to make a painful effort:

"What do you expect me to say to you? Do you think that because I am a priest I know more than you? I have my concerns like everybody does and I am no cleverer than anyone else. If you were asking me a question about bees, I could give you an answer," he said as he brushed away two that were climbing up his sleeve. "I have learned a great deal from bees and the miracle of honey still continues to amaze me. If God exists, He is in the honey! This is what I have discovered during my sixty-nine years, and my fifty years of ministry. The thought that through the repeated labours of thousands of insects, which could be crushed between two fingers, the pollen of flowers is changed into this golden nectar that sweetens life, and which encapsulates all the scents of the earth, the smells of plants and those of the winds – that is what confirms in me the idea that God exists, even if today many people attempt to convince us otherwise or try to impose something else, through fighting, assassination, bombs and blood. As for everything else, and these poor Negroes in particular, what do you expect me to say to you?"

"Why do you call them 'Negroes'?" said the Teacher indignantly.

The Priest looked up, searching for him through the dirty lenses of his spectacles. He found him eventually, and shrugged.

"So what do you want me to call them?"

"Blacks, Africans, men!"

"Will that be enough to bring them back to life?"

"It would be more dignified, at least. The word 'Negro' is an insult, you know that very well!"

"Not from my lips, Mr Teacher. Not from my lips. I am much older than you. I come from another time, after all. It was the word used when I was a child. A time when they spoke to me at school about Redskins, Yellow People, Whites and Negroes. That is how I learned about the world. It didn't stop us respecting them. Every man of each of these colours is a child of God. Hatred and contempt do not reside in the words, but in the use we make of them. But if you wish me to call these men 'Blacks', I will say 'Blacks'. I will do that if it pleases you and makes you happy. It won't make them any less dead."

The Teacher waved his hand in irritation. A bee landed on the knuckle of his thumb and, curling up, was about to sting him. He waved it away with his other hand. It fluttered unsteadily as far as the collar of the Priest's cassock. The Teacher resumed, somewhat wearily and sulkily, like a frustrated child:

"You haven't answered my question."

"I'm about to, don't worry: what the Mayor has said is not stupid, and God is my witness that I am not always in agreement with him, particularly, as everyone knows, over this costly plan for a spa that will bring us more luxury, corruption, false values and debauchery than exist already. But it would be worse still if our land were brought to the malicious notice of the outside world, and if we were suddenly to become an object of a curiosity that could only do us harm, Mr Teacher.

"My view is that we have all been chosen by God to preserve the memory of these unfortunate people, the memory of their death and the memory of their lives, even though we are only aware of the outcome. We have been chosen by God to know this and to retain it within ourselves, like a secret cross which we must carry on their behalf, but also on behalf of the other members of our community.

"We must bear the burden and pain of this secret, which will weigh heavily on our lives, but enable those of others not to be troubled in the future. And so what I propose, Mr Mayor, is a common-sense solution. I myself do not see the difference between burying a man in our cemetery or in a chasm. There is nothing undignified about that."

The Teacher could no longer keep still, and was turning towards everyone for support, for backing, but he remained isolated.

"If it is decided that I should bury the bodies of these unfortunate people," the Priest continued, "even though it's true that we don't know what their religion was or even whether they had one, I will do it. I will do it as I would for any human being, because it's my priestly duty. And tell yourself, to remove your scruples or your fear, Mr Teacher, that when one of our fishermen dies at sea, he never takes his place in our cemetery, and that does not prevent us praying for him and for the repose of his soul, and the vast place in which he lies for ever; this sea that bathes us, feeds us and troubles us contains no less rubbish or junk than the chasms of the Brau that seem to frighten you so much. That is my opinion, with the help of God."

The Priest stopped speaking, but his final words were followed by a sudden groan, because, as he always did at the end of his sermon, he had tapped his fingers together, forgetting the fresh wounds, so inadequately treated, that studded them.

VII

THE TEACHER PROBABLY SLEPT BADLY THE FOLLOWING night, because when the Mayor put his proposal to the vote in the fishing warehouse, it was adopted almost unanimously, the one exception being his.

The Mayor then proposed that, together with Swordy, the Priest and the Doctor, he would supervise what, for want of another name, he could only call the burial, even though it was clear that the word stuck in his throat. He also included the Teacher because he realised, even before the latter had intervened, that he would ask to be there. The Old Woman, who had hitherto been silent, remained so, and America must have been very glad to have been forgotten. This whole business had already taken up too much time. He had other things to do than deal with the funerals of savages.

After a final word from the Mayor, each of them set off into the night.

That being said, nobody slept easily that night, for the wind continued to blow its dank breath beneath the thresholds of house doors and through the poorly insulated window joints, setting their nerves, which were already as entangled as vipers, on edge. Of course, it was not just the wind that played on their minds: the image of the corpses of the three drowned men was stitched to the inside of their eyelids. No-one could be rid of it.

The Doctor woke up suddenly at 02:13 in the morning, as could be ascertained from his radio alarm clock and its luminescent numbers, having felt what he believed to be a large cold hand on his back stroking his spine, and he saw in front of him a huge face with lips of a blue that was almost black trying to kiss him on the forehead.

He switched on the television. This was not something he did very often nowadays. A politician was speaking. He was in his sixties, bronzed and with gleaming teeth. The Doctor turned off the sound. The politician resembled all his smooth-talking colleagues with their heavily made-up complexions, their dyed or implanted hair, and their pretty, supple, well-fed, turkey-like necks that emerged from the collars of their eternally pale-blue shirts.

The Doctor lost himself for a moment in the man's face, which, basically, was no-one's face, but it allowed him to forget those of the dead "Negroes", as the Priest called them. It astonished him that politicians could talk like this in the middle of the night – who for, and why, after all? He did not have the courage to turn up the sound to discover anything further because he knew that none of them had anything to say, anything profound or profoundly essential to the state of the world, such as those matters that can be discovered in books, for example. But it was the job of these men to talk all the time, to talk and never to listen to whoever was speaking to them, to never stop talking themselves, to live in the word, even the most meaningless of them, and one that becomes an ill-considered, cajoling noise, the modern-day siren song.

He heated up the coffee that was left in the saucepan on the cooker and drank it very black and without sugar, listening to the sound of the wind. He lit a cigar and picked up his old copy of Dante's "Inferno", which was never very far from him and had accompanied him over so many years. He opened it at random and, in a low voice, read ten or more lines, making the rugged words written almost a thousand years ago in a sequence that had not altered since then resonate, whereas so many things – monuments, empires, palaces, men, states, monarchs, beliefs – had vanished.

The Doctor smoked and read the verses aloud, just for himself, and also for the night which enveloped him like a warm shawl. He drank the coffee and a little marc as well. In small glassfuls. With great pleasure. The words and the smoke hovered in the air of his kitchen, and his thoughts did too, and for a brief and marvellous moment all three miraculously managed to come together and lure him into their immateriality, causing him to forget his overweight body, his age, the place where he happened to be and even who he was.

He remembered that as a child he would run around the narrow streets of the island, for he could run in those days, and he was able to forget about his body. He had the feeling that he was on his own, driven on by the excitement of what he was doing. His mind became a little devil feeding off the laughter and the thrills. He had no nostalgia for times past. He had no nostalgia: he hated looking backwards, because he did not recognise himself.

Alas, all pleasures come to an end: the coffee at the bottom of the cold cup suddenly developed a disgusting taste, the cigar, reduced to a few centimetres of tobacco wet with saliva, began to smell of piss and manure. The marc started to coat his oesophagus with a bitter taste. Only Dante stood upright, now and as he always did, taunting him with his words from a distant century. Inhuman, the words speak of the human. Like the Doctor's childlike soul, they float steadfastly and unconsciously above the bodies that run breathlessly, lifelessly, along the narrow, poorly paved streets of existence.

The Doctor went back to bed, feeling slightly sad but also comforted, without really knowing why.

VIII

TWO DAYS LATER, THE THREE DROWNED MEN HAD regained the warmth of the earth. The Mayor, the Doctor, the Priest, the Teacher and Swordy carried the frozen corpses, still wrapped inside the blue tarpaulin, from the cold room to the Mayor's small tracked vehicle that he uses for his vines, which are high up and far away.

It was still night-time. The sun would only rise in two hours. And so, walking at a slow pace, following the small vehicle – the only one on the island that is not pulled by animals, for there are neither roads nor cars here – they all set off for Nös di Boss, which is a large red rock overlooking a mass of fallen stones strewn there like bulky seeds by the idle hand of a Titan.

The last of the vines come to a halt a hundred metres lower down, and their stocks are so shrivelled and twisted that you can almost hear them complaining about having to dig their roots so deep, to find the small amount of water necessary for their survival. But it is also one of the vines on the island that provides the best grapes, in sparing and outstanding quantities. It belongs to Boueux, a cousin of the Mayor's who ineptly looks after road maintenance, a sluggish worker and an obese redhead, who is wedded to his two angora cats and only has one eye, the other having been lost in a brawl at the harbour during his turbulent younger days.

They took the small, dilapidated vehicle driven by Swordy to the very top of the dust track. The Mayor made the journey alongside his employee, and the Priest stood on the running board, next to the corpses, whose waters were breaking as though they were about to give birth. The Doctor, with his smile and his dyed moustache, struggled after them, on foot. As for the Teacher, he did not appear to be in the least affected by the effort, sustained as he was by his youthfulness, his physical shape and his sweet naïvety.

The pale light of dawn was rising when they left the vehicle at the furthest point of the track suitable for cars, where it rose in hairpin bends up the side of the volcano. In the distance, down below, was the blue expanse of the impervious sea.

The church bell, which could not be seen, was chiming seven o'clock. Neither could the little town be seen behind the jutting-out cliff. A large blood-red sun in the east was hesitating to leave the ocean. They carried the bodies on a stretcher, taking over from one another every fifty metres, in breathless silence. Only the Teacher, no doubt on account of his daily jogs, showed considerable energy. The others were too old and smoked too much, or they were too weak, too fat and not sufficiently motivated to make an effort.

In spite of the chilly air, they arrived at the first of the three holes dripping with sweat. The Doctor's smile now looked like a grimace and the dye from his moustache was dripping down on his lips in dark streaks. The others brushed the dust from their clothes and recovered their breath, every now and then glancing nervously into the hole. The blue tarpaulin was running with moisture and water was oozing into the plastic folds, falling to the ground in a rush of tears that were immediately consumed by the earth. They did not dare look at the bodies any longer; only a jumbled mass could be seen, the three corpses having been stacked together, which made the situation less human and all the more monstrous, but a monstrosity that was paradoxically reassuring, since it resembled a large sculpture.

The Mayor and the Teacher set off on their own to inspect the two other dark mouths of the crater, about a hundred metres away from the first one. The others sat down casually on the ground. None of them talked. Some smoked. The Priest took out his missal and his stole from the pockets of his cassock. A few bees also flew out and they began to circle their master's skull, providing him with an affectionate and noisy halo.

The two scouts returned: the Mayor declared that the hole situated highest up was certainly the one that offered the steepest entrance, so much so that neither he nor the Teacher had heard the pebbles they had thrown in bounce off the sides. There was a murmur of disappointment among the little group, because they had all hoped not to have to carry the load any higher, but they reconciled themselves with the task, and the procession began again, the Priest and his bees at the front this time, as if the sacred had invited itself on the walk from this point on, in order to take control.

When they finally arrived at the edge of the chasm, the mouth of which was only two metres wide, each of them wanted to look down into it, and they all observed that nothing could be seen, that no sound came from it and that only a damp smell arose, like a whiff of musty tobacco from the bowl of a pipe. The light had dimmed during the day, which seemed never to have dawned, and the sun had dissolved in the sea covered with a heavy charcoal sheet. It was also colder. And the sweat on their foreheads and beneath their armpits caused them all to shiver. They needed to get the business over quickly, otherwise they would well and truly catch their death there.

Swordy and the Teacher placed the load at the very edge of the hole. They gathered in a semi-circle. The Priest blessed the tarpaulin which Swordy gazed at sadly, a lovely, brand-new tarpaulin and one that might have been put to good use for years, as America had said, insisting that he be reimbursed, whereupon the Mayor had told him to shut his trap, that he would pay him for his bloody tarpaulin, out of his own money if necessary, and America, like a right ass, had said nothing and remained bitter, and at that moment Swordy, who did not like waste, probably thought that the three corpses did not need this fine tarpaulin to make their final journey and that by getting rid of things that were useful to the living in this way and were of no use to the dead they were just adding a second sin to the first.

The Priest said the prayer, skipping one word in every three. They made the sign of the cross. The bees also seemed to pause for reflection by flying around in silence. Then the Priest blessed the blue plastic once more, from which water now flowed as if from the spout of a fountain. It only remained for everything to be shoved into the hole. Swordy got down to the task, encouraged by the Mayor. The Doctor, who had recovered his breath, wedged his first cigar of the day between his teeth and lent a symbolic hand. The Teacher helped them too. They had to push hard, because the bundle clung to the roughness of the ground.

The three dead men who had come from elsewhere did not want to leave the world. Nearly all of them prepared to get ready, under orders from the Mayor, who organised the shove: "One, two, three!"

Then at last the blue tarpaulin toppled into the hole, accompanied by a silky sigh and by some bees that swarmed after it, abandoning the Priest and the others to their solitude. They flattened themselves against the edge of the sombre rim, side by side, out of breath, and peered into the darkness. They listened. They heard nothing. You could have thought that the three corpses were falling into infinity, without ever crashing into a ledge, a ridge or even the bottom of the chasm. You could also believe that they had never existed. That you had been dreaming up fantastical and macabre images in the uncomfortable hollow of a bad night, after having drunk too much wine, or eaten too much meat and gravy. You might have believed a lot of things that would have allowed you to live more happily afterwards.

IX

THE DAYS THAT FOLLOWED WERE A CONTINUAL COMEDY in which, it must be admitted, everyone played his or her part without the slightest false note. That is to say they all continued to carry out the scenes and actions of everyday life as they always had done: every morning, the Old Woman walked her dog at the same time and at the same place, crossing the black pebble beach, as she had done for years, without showing the slightest emotion when she passed by the place where the bodies had been washed up. The dog behaved like a dog, running ahead, tearing back again, chasing the seagulls or the waves, yapping for no reason and obeying when his mistress called him to heel. America tended his vines and did some building work for various people.

It would also soon be the time for the S'tunella, the great offshore tuna-fishing event on the island, and all the fishermen, Swordy included, were busy preparing the large nets, scrubbing the hulls and decks of the boats, and refuelling them for the operation during which three-quarters of the year's profits were at stake.

As for the Priest, he prepared his hives for the winter and continued to say mass in his church for three religious zealots and a dozen bees that appeared to be intoxicated by the fumes of incense, because their buzzing became excessive, before spending his afternoon in the harbour café, in his customary place at the very back of the room, where he read his breviary, his beekeeping manuals and the sporting press, being particularly keen on the results of the women's high jump competitions, a subject on which he was inexhaustible. He often tried to convince people that the graceful ascent of young athletes was a modern version of the assumption of the Virgin, and that God had created the high jump so that sinners could come closer to Him.

As for the Mayor and the Doctor, they met every evening at one or another's home, to go through the thick folder for the Spa. The final decision was to be made by the Consortium at the beginning of January, after a last visit. The Mayor wanted to welcome his investors in the best circumstances, anticipating their reservations and wishing to have all the arguments available to sweep them away.

The Teacher was the only one who was unhappy with his job as a teacher. Of course, he took care of his class conscientiously, a class of almost thirty children aged from six to twelve years old, but he did not do just this, as Swordy reported back to the Mayor after the latter had asked him to keep an eye on him. He went running in the morning, in his ridiculous outfit, but he interrupted his run to inspect the beach when he passed by. He approached the water's edge and walked slowly along the three hundred metres that made up the shoreline. He stopped occasionally, scanned the horizon, bent down to pick up an unidentifiable object which he eventually threw back into the water, and inspected the waves as though he was trying to work something out.

"How do you mean, work something out?"

"I don't really know," said Swordy, who was standing in front of the Mayor in the warehouse office, and was fiddling with his hat as though he were trying to unravel it. "It's as if he were searching. As if the waves were going to tell him something."

The Mayor stooped over the table for a few seconds. You would have thought his cares were weighing down on his shoulders. On the other side of the office windows, it was break time. The fishermen were rolling cigarettes or making coffee. No-one was looking in the direction of the office. Swordy was standing to attention in front of his boss. He did not know whether he should stay or go.

"What do you expect the waves to be saying to him, apart from singing the song of the sea?" said the Mayor eventually, in a thoughtful voice. "The sea doesn't speak."

Swordy nodded. He worked on the principle that one should always agree with one's boss. It was the best way of avoiding trouble. He also applied this to his wife, whom he had married for her gentleness and her beauty, but who, twenty years and three children later, resembled a grouper fish with a rasping voice.

"You can go."

The fisherman did not need telling twice and left the office. The Mayor was not at ease. The worm was entering the fruit. Without really knowing the Teacher, he suspected that his silence ever since the burial of the bodies concealed a particular purpose. But what was it?

It was always the same with men who had studied. The Mayor

reckoned that if the world was turning out so badly, it was the fault of men like the Teacher, bogged down in ideals and kindness, who search obsessively for an explanation of the how and the why, who convince themselves they should know right from wrong, good from evil, and who believe that the borders between the two aspects are like the cutting edge of a knife, whereas experience and good sense teach one that these borders do not exist, that they are merely a convention, a human invention, a way of simplifying what is complex and of getting some sleep.

The Doctor had also studied, and at some length, before returning to the island and taking the place of the Sad Fellow, who was more of a bonesetter than a doctor, and who dragged his melancholia around like a large, cumbersome piece of baggage, moaning to his patients about his own misfortunes. But he did not bore the pants off anyone with any of this, even though his house was full of books, and books that he read too, and this was what was most incredible to the Mayor. When the two of them, after having worked for a long time on the Spa project dossier, chewed on their cigars and knocked back small glasses of marc, the Doctor did not bore the Mayor with how he was feeling or with his views on Society, the State, Justice or these kinds of big words. They talked about fishing and the sky, vines and orchards, recalling moments of the childhood they had shared, strolling across the years like friends who have been nourished on the same air, the same dishes and the same odours.

These moments soothed the Mayor, who worried about everything and for whom responsibility often seemed to be a punishment, a punishment that he had not chosen, however, and which added to his own problems all those of the community.

One evening, after they had reviewed the compulsory purchases necessary for the project and assessed the amount of compensation and sales figures once more, the Doctor, as he poured the marc into their glasses, warned the Mayor:

"I really do need to tell you this. I have been informed that the Teacher wished to hire a boat."

"A boat?"

"A boat."

The Mayor put down his glass without having drunk from it.

"Who told you this?"

"A patient. I won't tell you which one. You know very well that we doctors are like priests. We listen and we say nothing."

"A small boat?"

"No. A proper boat. With a motor. A vessel that can put out to sea, reasonably far, safe and solid. With navigational instruments, a radio, sonar, GPS, and also a small cabin in which to sleep. Those are his words, apparently."

"And to do what? To fish?"

"To conduct some experiments."

"Some experiments?"

"I'm repeating what the person told me."

The Mayor's evening was ruined. He put down his glass and stubbed out his cigar, which had suddenly given him a pain in the throat. It was the word "experiment" that particularly upset him. It smelled bad, that word. It stank. It tasted of rot, like tooth decay caused by a fibre of meat that sticks in the mouth and goes bad.

He went home, giving the excuse that he was tired and had not slept all night, starting up from bed like scabbardfish do when they are trapped in the net. His wife suggested a cup of verbena tea, but he refused. She shrugged and went back to sleep. She slept like a dormouse.

What was this rascal up to? What could he mean by wanting to experiment? Of course, it had to do with the three corpses, but the Mayor failed to see the connection between what had happened and the hiring of a boat.

When the dawn light shone through the slits of the shutters, he was still tossing all this over in his head. He was not seeing things more clearly, but he had come to a decision all the same: the Teacher who loved sport so much could go and whistle for a boat. No-one would agree to lease him one. He would see to that.

It was not difficult for the Mayor to spread the word, particularly since the fleet was quite small, and all the boats would be required for the S'tunella, which was about to take place. There were, however, a few dinghies that either belonged to elderly fishermen who no longer went to sea but continued to maintain them in order to pretend that they still did, or to deceive themselves, or to tell themselves that it could still be possible and that where there was a will there was a way; or else they belonged to widows who saw in the boat on the quayside the image of their dead husbands, the extension of his forever absent flesh, and who would not dream of selling it for anything in the world, even if they had to live in poverty for the rest of their lives.

Sell it, no, but hire it out perhaps?

The Mayor paid some visits. They did not take long. At lunchtime he pushed open the door of the harbour café. He was smiling. He stood a round of drinks for all those present. He had obtained what he wanted. It had not been difficult. A few little promises, two or three banknotes, and then occasionally, when that had not been enough, a reminder that the Teacher was not from these parts. That he was not born on the island. That he was not like them. You only had to listen to him or look at him. It was the best argument, all in all, one that had to do with birth, the community and where you came from. That is how civilisations have been constructed and strengthened.

The Teacher sensed fairly quickly that a watchword had been given. When doors closed, or mouths clamped shut, or even when neither of them opened in the first place, he did not persist, but neither did he give up his plan. So it was that he was seen one Saturday, stepping aboard the ferry that made the crossing twice a week between the island and the mainland. His wife and his twin daughters accompanied him as far as the landing stage. He was holding a small travel bag that suggested a brief absence. In any case, he had school from Tuesday onwards, Monday that week being a holiday commemorating an armistice day, long ago.

The day was bright and the temperature very mild. It felt as though summer was trying its luck again. The Teacher kissed his wife and little girls, then he climbed on board. He could be seen walking straight to the main salon, which was empty, to sit down, putting his baggage beside him and opening the notebook in which many people imagined he wrote poems.

The captain sounded the horn and gave the order for departure and soon the weighty mass of the black-and-orange-painted vessel caused the harbour waters to bubble, and off it sailed for the mainland whose shores were never visible, but which one knew were there, towards the north-east.

X

THEY WERE EXPECTING TO SEE THE TEACHER ARRIVE BACK early on Tuesday morning, on the same ferry, but there was no sign of him. He had returned the day before, on Monday evening, when the twilight was already dimming the rays of sunshine that were sinking into the harbour waters.

No-one immediately realised that it was him, when they saw a boat they did not recognise and which, after an awkward manoeuvre, managed to dock at one of the two jetties. The pilot switched off the engine. His silhouette could be made out bustling around for a brief while in the narrow cabin, and it was only when he emerged and climbed up onto the bridge to cast out the mooring ropes and secure them, that people recognised the Teacher.

The name of the boat was *Argus*, and one might ask oneself whether it was not this name that had attracted the Teacher, who must have known his mythology.

He was not wealthy enough to have bought it or even to have hired it for the year, and the manner in which he attempted to dock the boat against the jetty several times before succeeding proved that he was not a skilful sailor. It was also noticed that, in the place where nets and crates are normally kept, the boat contained something quite different, some impressive white objects laid next to one another, but before they could be identified the Teacher had already closed the hatch, which he locked with a padlock.

From that day onwards, and until the end of September, the Teacher stopped running and devoted all his free time to sailing, particularly at the weekend, when he would be away for a couple of days, on his own, leaving his wife and two little daughters on the island. Of course, some fishermen in their boats happened to observe him moored in various places, scanning the skies with his binoculars, or they came across him at sea, but in a different place each time, so that no logical or recognisable intention could connect them.

The Mayor, to whom this was passed on, no longer slept as a result. Eventually he summoned the Teacher, as he had a right to do, since the school was answerable administratively to the community and he was, although not his immediate superior, nevertheless his employer and his landlord, as it were. In order that the interview should be less formal and so that the Teacher, who had an emotional nature, should not feel as if he was caught in a trap, the Mayor invited him to his home. He received him in what is called "the beautiful room", not because of its actual beauty, but because of its size, for it is the largest room in any of the houses.

The Mayor never set foot in it. When he worked with the Doctor, he preferred the kitchen, which reminded him of his mother and his grandmother, both of whom he had loved so much and whom he still often thought of with happiness. The beautiful room, on the other hand, conjured up death, because it was there, on the olivewood table covered for the occasion with a white cloth, that the bodies of the dead were habitually placed, after they had been washed, dressed and had their hair combed.

However much his wife polished the table every week – which created a smell of soft, warm wax in the confined space – and laid out on her tray the marital soup tureen, a bunch of dried flowers, and a few pink and gold trinkets that for some represented angels and for others dolphins, as well as some swallows and a couple of young shepherds whose colour varied according to the humidity, the Mayor could not stop himself seeing on the table the remains of his father, who died when he was only thirteen, from what was called at the time an "attack".

An artery had probably burst, unleashing a flow of blood that had streamed through his entire body and beneath his skin, as far as his face. In a flash, his face had turned scarlet, a colour that he had retained in death, so that when he was laid on the table his deceased father's ruddy complexion gave the impression that he harboured within him an anger that threatened to strike the child at any moment.

The Mayor asked the Teacher to sit down in one of the two armchairs whose backrests were covered with embroidered doilies. He suggested a cup of coffee or a drink, but his guest refused both. The Mayor noticed that the Teacher was nervous, and this amused him. And so he took his time, asking him for news of his wife and his daughters, then conversing with him about the strange weather and the heat that had returned, even leaving him on his own for a moment, offering the excuse that, due to a temperamental prostate, he often had to go to the lavatory, which was absolutely untrue.

When he returned, the Teacher's anxiety had increased still more.

"Supposing we talk a little about your fine boat?" said the Mayor with a smile.

"Ah, so that's it! Is that why you asked me to come here?"

"Are your 'experiments' conclusive?"

"When they are, you shall be the first to be informed, Mr Mayor."

"May we know what type of thing they are?"

The Teacher seemed astonished by the persistence of the man who was addressing him. He was about to mumble something, hesitated and probed the Mayor's expression. It seemed to have shrunk. His body had faded still more. All that remained were his eyes, which shone with an intense and steady brilliance and were searching the Teacher's face, like crochet hooks, as though trying to get inside him, to cut open his skin, to bore into his bones, to break viciously into his skull and to swoop into his brain matter so as to latch on to his thoughts.

"I'm surprised your spies have not informed you yet."

The Mayor did not react to the cutting remark. The Teacher breathed more easily. The phrase had cost him a great deal. He was still blushing from it.

"That's not an answer," the Mayor said, determined not to let him off.

"I've nothing to hide, after all. I work by daylight. I study the currents."

"The currents?" said the Mayor, smiling again.

"The currents. I want to understand how the corpses of those men could have washed up on the island's beach. It defies all logic."

"Because according to you it's logic that controls the seas?"

"I'm talking about physical logic: if an object is thrown into the water at such and such a place, the marine currents will carry it to a specific other place. The currents are known. They only have tiny variations, depending on the season, as I don't need to tell you. I have repeated the journey the smugglers make, who, for crazy amounts, promise these men to take them to the mainland. I have dropped dummies along the route, at different points, ten in all. None of them has washed up on the beach until now. None."

"The sea sometimes takes its time. Its rhythm is not man's rhythm," objected the Mayor, who had stopped smiling. "That being said, I don't understand what you're trying to prove."

The Teacher allowed himself to smile for the first time. He was breathing as though he had just been running for a long while, and was wringing his hands. The Mayor waited. This man was not made as he was. This man was a lunatic, ruled by his sensitivity, and enslaved by it. He would persevere to the end. He was certain of this now, and had just reached this conclusion: nothing could stop him. The Teacher probably saw it as a sort of mission. A higher objective that enabled him to forget his wretched and temporary condition, his tiresome and not very rewarding job, his dreary life?

He was the type of man who, during the wars, left the trenches in a standing position, shouting as he dragged others along, taking no notice of the bullets that were whistling around him and mowing bodies down. He was also the type of man who could not kill a fly in his day-to-day life, but who, in the course of revolutions, had sent his fellow men to the scaffold without batting an eyelid. He was the type who was still wrapped up in childhood and its fantasies, but who, in the name of a belief, could without a qualm massacre those who did not subscribe to it. His type was not made for the world of men, which is the product of flexibility, compromise and concessions. This kind of man could only create idiots, martyrs or torturers. And the Mayor had not the slightest intention of being used as a victim.

"You'll know soon enough. Allow me to take my leave now. I have to prepare my lessons for tomorrow."

The Teacher did not wait for the Mayor to reply. He had already got to his feet and said goodbye in a somewhat theatrical manner, struggling to conceal the trembling that gripped his lips and his hands. He looked like a tall, very gentle boy trying to stop himself from crying after something or other had upset him. He left.

The Mayor remained seated for a long while in his armchair, pensive and feeling irritated. The seconds ticked by on the clock beside him, making the sound of wood being chopped. This made him think of a tiny woodcutter, tireless and like a metronome, busily and invisibly pursuing his task. Then his wife's voice came from the kitchen. She was calling him to lunch. He was not hungry. The Teacher had taken away his appetite.

XI

ON FRIDAY THE 28TH AND SATURDAY THE 29TH OF September, two noteworthy events occurred which got on the nerves of some people even slightly more: on Friday, at about midday, two children found one of the Teacher's dummies on the beach. Not knowing who it belonged to, they informed the first adult they encountered: it was the Priest. He was returning from his beehive, carrying the honey he had gathered in two buckets.

He accompanied the children to the beach, and, with his weak eyesight and his maladjusted spectacles, when he noticed the dummy he thought for a moment that it was a sort of pagan idol. He held up the crucifix of his rosary in front of the object, made the sign of the cross and trotted off a prayer, inviting the children to join in with him.

The two boys, slightly more aware than the Priest, drew his attention to the fact that it was a simple floating dummy of the kind used in swimming pools for training top swimmers and lifeguards. A human-sized torso, as heavy as a body, made of plastic trimmed with lead. When they turned it over, they realised that a message had been written on it saying that if the object was discovered, one was requested to advise someone whose name was written on the dummy's torso, which was that of the Teacher. His address was there too. On the dummy's stomach there was another number, in Roman numerals: IX.

The Teacher was still sitting at table with his wife and little daughters when the two children knocked on his door. The Priest told anyone who cared to listen to him afterwards that, when they told him about their discovery, the Teacher's face was transformed and that he, without even waiting for the end of their story, set off running towards the beach, even forgetting to take off the napkin that he had tucked into his collar so as not to dirty his shirt.

The two children went away. The Priest and his bees remained on the doorstep a little while longer. The Teacher's wife and little girls appeared, their eyes filled with questions. The Priest summarised what had happened. The wife let out a long sigh.

"The dummies are the only things that matter to him. I don't know what's come over him. I no longer recognise him."

"I don't believe I've ever seen you at church," said the short-sighted Priest, who had drawn close to the woman's face and was trying to scrutinise her. A bee had landed on one of the twins' arms. It was wending its insect's path over her fresh, young skin. The little girl was not frightened. Quite the contrary, with her forefinger she gently began to stroke the downy back of the tiny creature, which curiously enough did not appear to mind.

"I don't believe in God," the woman replied in a flat voice, which the Priest read as regret.

"That's a great shame. He can be of such help."

"Who told you that I'm in need of help?"

"Who would dare have the pride to assert that they do not need it?"

Then the conversation took on a more mundane turn, for the Priest had long ago given up all attempts to convert atheists. Religion wearied him. He himself, it was thought, did not believe in it very strongly. He continued to behave as though he did in order not to leave the last of the flock on their own, people whom he had nevertheless shocked one day by telling them in a sermon that God had retired.

"It's not just the clerks in the ministries of the capital who want to work at seventy per cent when they feel old age coming on. I rather think that God has done the same. He's progressively suspended all activity. And it's our fault."

Two elderly ladies had left the church amid a clattering of chairs. One of them even denounced the Priest and his blasphemy to the bishop in a letter covered in mistakes and holy water. But the bishop probably had other lost souls to get excited about and the sanctimonious creature never received a reply.

The Priest could not resist giving the two little girls a brief course in beekeeping. He took his leave after having poured a little of his honey in a bowl which he had asked one of the girls to fetch for him.

Returning from the beach, the Teacher walked quickly, in spite of the dummy he clasped in his arms rather like a dancing partner. He still had his napkin around his neck. America caught up with him with his donkey and cart. He invited the Teacher to climb up with his contraption. The sun illuminated the scene and from the surrounding vines there arose the sweet scent of bunches of grapes that were slowly drying on the stone walls.

"I'm almost home. It's alright. Thank you."

"Are you going to marry her? At least that one won't be a bloody nuisance!"

The Teacher did not react to the joke and left America alone with his laughter. The latter rolled along in silence alongside the Teacher, who was beginning to show signs of weariness, then he shrugged and whipped the back of the donkey which, without complaining, set off at a light trot.

Several pupils in the class reported that the Teacher was not himself that afternoon. He gave them all a task to be carried out in silence that was so long that the youngest eventually began to doze off at their desks and the older ones became bored and started to daydream.

During the break he forgot about them, leaving them on their own in the yard making a terrible din, not even aware of the racket, so absorbed was he in writing whatever it was, though it was probably not poetry, in his little notebook, all the while glancing from time to time at the dummy that he had propped up near his desk in a corner of the classroom, beneath the blackboard, and measuring distances on a large sea chart he had spread out in front of him.

He worked late that evening. Swordy reported to the Mayor that the light had remained on in his house until two o'clock in the morning.

"I got frozen outside in the alleyway."

"I'm paying you for that."

"With respect, you're paying me to fish for something."

"Then tell yourself that it's a type of angling. Would that make you feel better?"

Swordy said nothing and tried to understand what the Mayor had just said. Nobody made any comments. It was Saturday. It was early. Seven o'clock. The Mayor had invited the Old Woman, the Priest, America and Swordy to the Doctor's house. They were all there. They were sitting down in the waiting room. The Doctor joined them. He was carrying a tray on which he had put out cups of coffee. He was smiling, as he usually did, for he never lost his smile, even when he was announcing an incurable disease or the approach of death. It was like a mask. No-one really knew what lay behind it.

"Well," began the Mayor, grimacing after having gulped down the boiling hot coffee and replaced his cup on the tray, "if I have asked you to come, it's because I have need of you. Need of you, so as to understand."

Following this introduction, and continuing to grimace so that one began to wonder whether it was the very hot and very strong coffee that was responsible for the words issuing from his mouth, he itemised the activities of the Teacher during the past three weeks, going back over aspects that everybody knew already, adding others that were known only to some of them and which they themselves had reported to him. He concluded with the events of the previous day, the dummy washed up on the beach, the afternoon at the school, the Teacher's intense writing activity, his lateness to bed. Swordy let out a long sigh, as if to substantiate this last point.

"That is where we are," he concluded, clenching his fists and hammering on his spindly thighs.

Then there was silence. The room had filled with the slightly sickly smell of coffee-filled breath.

"You say that you need us in order to understand, but you're not telling the truth."

It was the Old Woman who had spoken, in her gravelly voice,

which all those who were present that morning – with the exception of the Priest, who at a young age had been sent to the mainland to a school for priests – were familiar with from their long childhood years, when it had made them tremble.

"You're crafty," she went on. "You always have been. You don't need us in order to understand, just to share."

"Share? Share what?" barked the Mayor, overplaying his amazement.

"Your burden. What you want is not for us to help you understand, but for us to help you bear it. You are relying on us to comfort you."

Swordy and America stared at one another. All this was beyond them. It was philosophising. It hurt the head more than the worst hangovers. The Doctor was smiling and sipping his coffee. The Priest was gazing at the ceiling. He seemed completely uninvolved with what was going on.

"You're talking nonsense!" snapped the Mayor.

"Don't make fun of me. You know very well what I mean. You don't want to be on your own. You prefer us all to drown together. You want to take us with you. By telling us everything you know, you're making us accomplices."

"No crime has taken place, as far as I know!"

"Not yet. But there have already been three deaths."

Suddenly, at the same moment, a hum ran through the waiting room. It was like the rumble of a train arriving in the distance, advancing slowly but growing gradually louder, seeping into the walls, into the ground, creeping into the legs of the chairs, climbing up their spines so as to enter the bodies that were seated there and spread a muted vibration through them. At the same moment, the cups that had been replaced on the tray started to tinkle and the tray itself seemed to come alive as though the spirit of a dead waiter was trying to pick it up to take to the kitchen. The Priest made the sign of the cross and began to murmur a prayer. The others did not appear surprised or frightened. They waited. The sound rumbled on for ten seconds or so, then stopped.

The Brau had returned to its slumber.

"It's been a long time!" said America, who was more embarrassed by the silence than by the quaking earth.

"Fourteen months and three days," stated the Doctor, who kept a scrupulous record – solely for the record, not to get anything out of it or for his edification – of the shudders of the volcano. Then, in an abrupt switch, he returned to the original conversation.

"We cannot deny the Teacher's responsible attitude and his perseverance. He is a knowledgeable man, and it is right that he should look for ways of perfecting his knowledge, of throwing light on dark areas. That the Teacher should try to understand why the bodies of these men have been washed up on our island is, after all, his right. What would be awkward is if he felt like sharing his discoveries, writing them down, slipping them into an envelope and sending them away."

"Who to?" the Mayor asked.

"To people other than us."

"Why would he do that?" said Swordy. This early morning conversation, in the waiting room that had always been a place he did not care for and was synonymous with injuries and pains of all kinds, was making him ill.

"Out of vanity," said the Priest.

"Out of pride," said the Old Woman.

"Out of stupidity," said the Mayor.

"Out of innocence," said the Doctor.

America was the only one not to say anything. Swordy turned to him, expecting a comment to complete the outburst, but no comment came. America merely held out his empty palms in a gesture of impotence. Swordy looked at the encrusted lines of cement and dirt to be seen on them. He remembered that certain clairvoyants foretold the future by reading palms. He tried to do so, but all he saw were lines, hatches and geometrical forms crushed one against the other. Chaos. Confusion. Nothing at all, really.

They parted without having made progress and without having decided anything either. But what was there to decide upon? The Old Woman was probably not wrong in the remarks she had made to the Mayor. He certainly wanted to make them feel that they were all united with one another, and that even though some time had elapsed since their macabre discovery, these same bodies still pressed down on them like a cast-iron weight. Not one of them wished to endure the embarrassment on his or her own. They all needed to share the burden.

XII

MID-MORNING OF THAT SAME DAY, IN MID-MORNING, the ferry entered the port, having blared out its siren three times as usual as it approached.

There were few passengers: some local inhabitants who had gone to deal with business matters on the mainland and were returning home; Pill, who worked for the pharmacy and suffered from a club foot and a liverish complexion, who delivered the Doctor's weekly order to him; two elderly ladies who were nicknamed the Sisters, without anyone actually knowing if they really were, who came every year at the same time to visit one of their cousins and stayed until Christmas; and also a middle-aged stranger, neither tall nor short, neither fat nor thin, neither young nor old, who appeared to be the perfect embodiment of ordinariness, one of those men whom people never notice, whom waiters in cafés ignore in spite of their insistent raised finger, and whose existence women are unaware of even when they brush up against them.

The man was carrying a bag of the type that travelling salesmen used to have when travelling salesmen were still a breed that roamed the world.

He was the last to come down the gangway of the ferry, and then found himself on the quayside, taking stock of where he was. It was not hard to understand, from his expression and his slight hesitation, that he was setting foot on the island for the first time. When the man became aware that there was only one café in the port, and that his choice would therefore be limited, he set off towards it.

The few fishermen sitting at table were discussing the imminent S'tunella, their hopes for it, their calculations, and the exact moment they should set off, for each of them was still waiting for the signal for departure.

Every year, this signal is given by a small, unofficial group, made up of the oldest fishermen on the island, who gather one day without actually being consulted at the far end of the jetty, on the last bench facing the sea, just as certain animals that carry on age-old rituals of love, hunting and death congregate in certain places, guided by their blood, their instincts and their desires.

People were waiting for this moment. When they were seen making their way towards the bench, which no-one here would have dared to occupy at this time, the atmosphere of the town filled with electric particles. They were watched from afar, even with binoculars at times. People murmured. They tried to guess what they could be saying to one another. They awaited their decision, which they delivered with marked succinctness and an effective sense of abbreviation, and which was enough to suddenly transform the little port, drowsy until then, into a vibrant space filled with cries, movement and colour.

The door was open. The man entered and greeted the customers, who stared at him without responding, which did not appear to upset him. In a corner at the back he noticed a priest wearing a cassock, his head bent over a sports newspaper that he was trying to read through thick-lensed spectacles as he gently waved away some bees that in turn fluttered about and settled, like aeroplanes in large, crowded airports, on the pages of the newspaper. The man walked over to the bar and set down his bag by his feet.

"A glass of the local wine."

Only a foreigner speaks like this. An inhabitant of the island would never express himself in this way. He would simply ask for a glass of wine, because the only wine served here is the wine of the island. Everyone would refuse to drink any other. It is a matter of honour.

The Café Owner said nothing. He grabbed a glass and a bottle. He poured the wine into the glass, and the man seemed to appreciate its almost black amaranth colour. He put down a banknote that he had taken from his trouser pocket and sniffed the wine before tasting it.

The customers as well as the Café Owner lost interest in him and went back to what they had been doing, the customers to their whispered conversations, the Café Owner to his accounts, which he was working on in some pain, to judge by his anxious brow and the pencil that he chewed between his yellow teeth. The man took his time drinking his wine, and when he had finished it, he ordered another glass. When the Café Owner came over to him again with the bottle, the man told him that he was looking for a room for a few days. He had things to do here.

"To do with the Thermal Baths project?" asked the Café Owner.

"The Thermal Baths? Yes, indeed," the man replied, "the Thermal Baths, obviously. What else?"

He sensed that nothing further was needed to reassure the person he was addressing.

"There's no hotel on the island, but if you're not fussy, I have a room with a bed and a bathroom. It's just around the corner. I can show it to you."

The man followed the Café Owner, who had taken a key from a panel behind the counter. They walked twenty metres or so, as far as a metal curtain which indicated that there had once been a shop here that had closed a long time ago.

"A haberdashery," the Café Owner explained to the man. "My mother used to run it. The shop didn't survive her. I've refurbished it inside. I let it occasionally, to seasonal workers who come for the capers harvest, or to fishermen, too, when there are not enough of our own men."

He drew back the curtain and opened the door that still had its bell. The room was square, the walls had been whitewashed. Two single beds, each against a wall, a small table by a window, over which hung a nylon curtain printed with a pattern of palm trees and pineapples, a cupboard in one corner and a door at the back, behind which were the lavatory and the washbasin. The floor was made up of large, uneven slabs of lava on which thousands of feet had trod. The damp at the bottom of the walls revealed some phosphorescent green atolls.

The only decoration was a photograph hung above one of the two beds. In black and white, within a watermarked and misshapen frame of gilded plaster, it depicted an elderly woman with her hair in a bun who squinted slightly.

"Will this do for you?"

"It will be perfect," said the man.

The Café Owner informed him of the price. The man insisted on paying a full week in advance.

"You can have breakfast in the café. I open early. As to meals, my wife cooks for some people. If you feel so inclined, you must tell me a bit in advance. I imagine you want to see the Mayor?"

"I was going to ask you about him."

"At this time you will find him in the town hall. His office is open. You take the first narrow street on your left as you leave. You go as far as the church, which you pass on your right. You reach a small square. The town hall is there. You can't get lost. In any case, there are the flags."

The Café Owner left. The man had told him that there would be no point in coming to tidy up. He would cope on his own. He put down his bag without opening it, sat down on a bed and lit a cigarette. From his pocket he took a flat silver-plated flask and took a long swig. He smoked as he looked at the photograph. He continued to gaze at it and, having stubbed out his butt in a yellow ashtray provided by a brand of aperitif, he unhooked the frame and tossed it on top of the cupboard.

XIII

THE DOCTOR WAS THERE WHEN THE MAN ARRIVED AT THE town hall. The man greeted him and said hello to the Secretary. He wanted to talk to the Mayor and when she asked him in what capacity and why, he leaned over the counter that separated her from him and whispered a few words in her ear that the Doctor did not hear but which immediately caused her to adopt a solemn expression, to look at the visitor apprehensively and to walk over to the Mayor's office where she knocked three times, waited, checked her appearance, tucked in a fold of her blouse that had come away from her skirt, replaced her large breasts in the cups of her brassiere, patted her hair, turned towards the man, closing the door behind her once the Mayor had told her to come in.

A few seconds later, the Mayor emerged hurriedly from his office, the Secretary at his heels. He walked over to the man, holding out his hand, while displaying an anxious expression that he did not even attempt to conceal. He asked him to follow him. It was only then that he remembered the Doctor.

"We'll see each other later. I'll explain."

The man was a policeman, of a particular kind, working on

his own and without any real ties. Only discreet missions were entrusted to him, in the course of which he had total freedom of action. He was in a way his own boss and he had plenty of time. What mattered in his eyes and those of his superiors was success, and that always came with a price. The areas in which he intervened were often sensitive and needed tact and patience at one and the same time. The Mayor should not worry, he was not trying to persuade him that he belonged to some sort of secret service, not at all, and as if to prove it he took from his wallet a card on which there was a slightly faded and yellowing photograph of a young man who did not look the least like him but who must have been the Superintendent. He put the card away before the Mayor, who had nonetheless held out his hand, could take it and examine it.

"As you can see, a simple policeman. You are probably wondering what I am doing here among you?" the Superintendent asked the Mayor, who could feel his body growing taut and his heartbeat slowing down.

"Yes."

"You don't have the least idea?"

"No," gasped the Mayor, as he tried to maintain a neutral expression, but he was not gifted as an actor and even an idiot could have seen that a thousand thoughts were buzzing around in his head.

"Do you really not know?" the Superintendent persisted, putting the Mayor through agonies.

And as if to add to the councillor's torment still further, he stood up, and began to walk around the office a little, as if he were at home, and, actually, this aimless pacing about, this flowing walk, had no other purpose than to say just that, to make him realise that he was suddenly taking over, that it was he who would now be in charge and who would lead the dance into which he was getting ready to drag the Mayor, and with him the entire island, if he felt like it.

"Is your visit connected to the Thermal Baths project, perhaps?" the Mayor dared ask.

"The Thermal Baths? Ah yes, the Thermal Baths, people have already mentioned this to me. Let's agree, you and me, if it's simpler for you, that I am actually here for this project. My true purpose must not be known by all of your fellow citizens. You can introduce me in this way if you want to, but you don't in the least need to. I couldn't give a damn about your thermal plans, do you understand? I couldn't care less. I've always been appalled by it all. The idea of people taking the waters and walking around all day in bathrobes, drinking large glasses of warm water to get rid of the stink of rotten eggs, depresses me. But if that's what you want, much good may it do you! Develop your project! Transform your dying island into a clinic for chlorotic ghosts, it's got nothing to do with me. By the way, you wouldn't have something to drink, some wine, or something stronger? Yes, a stiff drink would be best. If you don't mind, of course."

Later on, when the Mayor went to see the Doctor to tell him about the interview, he admitted that he had wanted to strangle the Superintendent.

"He's like the fledgling crows we used to search for in nests when we were children, do you remember? Insignificant little creatures, pinkish, warm, without grace or beauty, vulnerable. We didn't expect them to be bad or malevolent, but remember how they started to peck until we bled when we picked them up? Well, this policeman, he's just like them. Beneath his appearance of a post office employee, he's a slumbering eel. He's going to make us sweat time and again, I tell you. We're not going to get rid of him easily. And his manners. I can't stand his manners, his voice, what he says. Do you know how he spoke about our island?"

The Mayor had eventually found a bottle of anisette in a drawer. He wondered how it could have got there, since he never drank it himself. He poured a glass for the Superintendent, and he put two drops in another glass, for himself, out of politeness. He could not bear this sticky drink, with its taste of fennel and medicine. They clinked glasses. The Superintendent tossed his back. He held out his glass again. The Mayor was obliged to refill it.

"I don't like water cures, as you have realised, but I don't like islands either. A large island is always too small for me. It's the very idea of an island that is unbearable to me. Being surrounded by water. I'm a continental person. In the morning when I get up I like to know that I only have to get into my car and drive and that, a few days, a few weeks later, I can be in Vienna, in Moscow, in Baku, in Delhi or, why not, Beijing. I only like solid ground. I don't like water, salty or fresh. I don't like islands. I don't like your island, which doesn't even have the excuse of being a large island. It could be taken off the maps, who would complain? All of you? But do you matter? A few hundred human beings out of seven billion. I leave it to you to work out the percentage. It's probably a thousand times less than the loss threshold they put up with in any industry. If I come here, it's out of necessity. But I don't like being here, just as I'm beginning to feel that I don't like you. Basically, there's not very much I do like. I don't like society. I don't like my country or the times I live in. I don't like human beings any more than I like any species of animal. The only thing that I like without reservation, intensely, obsessively, is my job. Yes, I like my job. And then drinking, too. Without being, strictly speaking, an alcoholic, I drink a great deal, and without ever getting drunk. My doctor can't understand it."

He drained his glass once more. He picked up the bottle. Served himself. Sat down with one buttock on the Mayor's desk.

"You probably find me badly brought up. Ill-mannered. Tell yourself that I really am and that I couldn't give a damn. I couldn't care less what you think or will think of me. I am not here to be liked. I am here to find a bone, to dig it up, to gnaw it a bit to discover the taste, and to take it away if I reckon it is needed by those who sent me here. But I'm annoyed that I have to be here. On an island. I wonder how anyone can live on an island, especially an island like yours, so wretched and so ugly. Dark, bleak, without beauty. I've never heard anyone talk about it, I tell you. It's the arsehole of the world, Mr Mayor. I've been told that mobile phones don't work, that there is no internet connection. I thought they were teasing me."

"It's because the island has been classified as a World Heritage Site. No aerial can be erected."

"Heritage Site my arse! A heritage site is beautiful! Human beings are beautiful! The men and women I've met since I arrived are all afflicted by a malformation, with squints, ears that stick out, or huge noses, limbs that are too long, weird teeth. The café owner I am staying with has six fingers on each hand. Six fingers! Have you ever seen such a thing before? They're degenerates! You, Mr Mayor, you look as though you're not quite perfect. You have the body of a child and the head of an old man."

The Mayor confessed to the Doctor, after knocking back his

glass of marc, that he had been within an inch of punching the man in the face. No-one had ever spoken to him like that since primary school and brawls in the playground. But he could not forget that the man was a policeman, and that even a mayor who has been insulted cannot give a hiding to a policeman, and what's more, one who was a superintendent.

"I preferred to persuade myself that I had misheard, or that he was totally drunk, despite what he had said. I controlled myself. I told him that in our arsehole of the world, as he called it, we were not actually cut off from everything. We have television."

"Big deal! Television! We're in the twenty-first century! Wake up! Do you think you can live cut off from the world? Well, as it happens it's the twenty-first century that brings me here."

Then the Superintendent launched into a frenetic tirade. He spoke to the Mayor for half an hour, draining the bottle of anisette, and the Mayor began to wonder what this maniac, who had stepped right out of a performance by a clown devised by a lunatic, was driving at.

"People never really know what they have above their heads. For thousands of years, they put God there. This suited them. They were down below. They sweated blood and tears. And up above, there was God on His cloud, who created them, watched over them, saved them or damned them. And then man thought he was clever. He got rid of God. Tossed Him in the dustbin. Spent a little while intoxicated by this minor murder he had performed, and then became aware of the void he had created. Man's unique characteristic is always to act too quickly. Always. It began to alarm him, all this empty space. He tried to heat up some old dishes, but everything had a burnt taste. At that point, he became really frightened. He took refuge in the only place that remained to him: Progress. Mind you, it has existed since time immemorial. Give a man fire, some iron and a hammer, and in a matter of seconds he will forge a chain to shackle another man who looks just like his brother and keep him on a leash, or use a spearhead to kill him, rather than make a wheel or a musical instrument. The wheel and the trumpet, they came later, much later than the chain and the spearhead, and in the meantime a great many people had already been slaughtered. And when the wheel was invented, it was only so that the slaughter could be taken further afield, like the sailing ship, so that the whole world could benefit from it, and the trumpet was only used to cover up the cries of those who were being murdered and to celebrate the butchery. Full stop. And today we have the satellites!"

The Mayor listened in astonishment to the man's long, angry diatribe, wondering whether he was dreaming, whether he was in a novel, whether it was the middle of the night and he was in his bed, with his wife beside him in her long pink nightdress, and her aroma of soap and lavender, and the wind from the sea humming in the narrow streets outside, in the throes of a nightmare such as he had from time to time and which left him dubious and pensive in the morning.

"I even pinched myself. But no, I was not asleep: I really was in my office with this insane person who had appeared from nowhere, who had left me in peace during the sixty years I have lived so far and whose existence I was thankfully unaware of, who was talking to me about satellites, who was trying to convince me that God, compared to satellites, is cat piss. That, thanks to the satellites, the notion of God has been raised by ten to the power of fourteen."

The Doctor was smiling. His smile made the Mayor feel even more irritated, even though he knew that this smile meant nothing. It did not mean that the Doctor was smiling at him. It was his own way of displaying his face, just as he, the Mayor, displayed his with an expression of continuous annoyance and noticeable irritation, including during those moments – rare, it's true – when he was happy and relaxed.

It has to be admitted that the Mayor was extremely patient with the Superintendent, not interrupting him at any point while he was delivering a verbal outpouring about power and the brilliance of satellites, in which scientific properties were merged with metaphysical meanderings. The earth was being tapped. The world under surveillance. Naïve and credulous men, idealistic and blind, were taking to the streets to demonstrate in democracies, against the restriction of basic freedoms, the right to a private life, and other bits of similar nonsense. They signed petitions, wrote opinion columns, questioned their members of parliament in this way, while the least of their actions and gestures, their movements, their remarks, were being observed at every moment, and it would require a great deal of money and political willpower that was not yet in evidence for the life of each one of them to be registered and for the tiniest details to be filed away. For practical purposes. One can imagine which ones.

Following this, the Superintendent, after a sad glance at the totally empty bottle of anisette that he had thrown in the waste-paper basket, came back and sat down opposite the Mayor, thrust his hand into his briefcase and pulled out a wad of twenty or so pages which he tossed onto the desk with a casual flick of his wrist.

"They were only photocopies. Photocopies of colour photographs. To begin with, I didn't understand a thing. On the first ones, there was some blue, some ochre strips with irregular contours, some darker points of unequal sizes, and some red lines that linked certain of these features. You would have thought it was a reproduction of an abstract painting.

"On the next ones, there was less blue and more dark points, some red lines and some very small dots circled in green. That's when I recognised the open jaw of the Dog. They were aerial shots, taken from his famous satellites no doubt, of the archipelago, of all the islands, and of our own of course, which I had never seen like that before, vertically, as though I had suddenly become that eye of God of which the Superintendent had spoken.

"Some of them are fiendishly precise. You can make out the vineyards, the houses, the church. You can see wine growers, peasants in the orchards, and groups of men and women at the harbour. Other photographs show boats at sea. I recognised some people who come from here, and there were others whom I didn't know."

The Mayor paused for a moment, gave the Doctor an irritated glance, knotted his fingers and resumed.

"And then there are boats that don't even deserve that name, like a sort of barge with a cargo that I originally took for timber, like planks pressed one against the other. You can't even see the cockpit. You have the sense that a barge was loaded and that it was launched without anyone bothering what would become of it afterwards. One of the photos of these small boats made me shudder because I suddenly understood: what I first took for planks were men. Men standing, or lying down, huddled together, crammed into old tubs, and some of these tubs were being towed by boats, by fishing boats."

The Mayor waited for the Doctor to react. For him to say something. For him to help him. But the Doctor remained silent, sipped his glass of marc and rolled a cigar between his plump fingers, pausing to light it, delaying a little longer the pleasure of drawing the flame to it, of inhaling the first puffs, of tasting the haze of warm smoke in his mouth which would leave its flavour of forests, of damp earth and dead leaves for a long time.

"You're not saying anything?"

"What do you expect me to say?"

"Do you understand, at least?"

"I think I'm beginning to understand."

"And doesn't that frighten you?"

The Doctor raised his eyebrows. Scratched his moustache which at this time of day, the very beginning of the afternoon, was still extremely black.

"Don't take it as bravado, but I don't know what could frighten me. Fear is a sensation I no longer experience. I'm not bragging about it. I didn't even have to make an effort for it to be like this. The last time I was frightened was when my wife was ill. And fear didn't help me at all. It didn't stop the illness. It didn't make my wife less unhappy. It didn't prevent her from suffering and it didn't relieve me of my grief when she died."

The Mayor was suddenly annoyed that the Doctor should mention his wife. He could once more see her gentle features, her large dark eyes in her pale face. He felt irritated by his own oversensitiveness, and continued angrily:

"But I'm not asking you whether you are frightened on your

own behalf! But whether you're frightened for our sake, for the community, for the island, for what we have done?"

The Doctor could not stand it any longer. He lit his cigar. He did so ceremoniously, for he considered it to be one of the most solemn things that existed in his life. A protocol, or a homage. Or both of them combined. He gave a few puffs, exhaled the smoke, and smiled even more.

"And why should I be frightened for our sake, as you say?"

"I don't believe you have really understood. I thought you had guessed. Do you know what is on one of these bloody photographs taken by his wretched satellites?"

"Judging by the way your eyes are trying to pop out of their sockets and your neck is swelling up, I'm going to know very soon."

"Well, we are there. All of us! That famous morning, on the beach! You can recognise us perfectly. As though one of the seagulls flying overhead had pressed the shutter release. It's frightening! You can make out the Old Woman, her dog, Swordy, America, me! Do you realise that these blasted things fly at hundreds of kilometres an hour in the sky and it's as though they were watching us through the keyhole! I can't get over it! Bloody hell!"

"And me?"

"What about you?"

"Can I be seen?"

"Of course you can be seen! Especially you, what's more! One can't miss you, you take up so much space. And at our feet, there is the tarpaulin."

"The tarpaulin?"

"The tarpaulin. The blue tarpaulin. America's tarpaulin. And it's quite obvious there is something underneath it."

"Can you make it out, this something?"

"No. But that doesn't mean a thing. He's probably got other photographs on the side, which he didn't show me. Who knows! This sort of guy doesn't reveal all his cards at once."

The Mayor stopped talking. The Doctor immersed himself in the smoke from his cigar. They remained like this for a long time, without saying anything further to one another, which was scarcely their usual habit.

XIV

WHAT TAUTENED THE ROPE STILL MORE THAT DAY TOOK place at the end of the Mass for the blessing of the boats, known colloquially as "the Tuna Mass", when the Teacher confronted the Mayor.

It is customary for the Priest to come to the port and for him to bless every boat that is due to depart for the S'tunella. In earlier times, this took the form of a solemn and sumptuous procession, which set off from the church in the early afternoon to the sound of the communal fanfare; each fishing boat with its crew placed itself under the protection of a male or female saint and maintained an altar to his or her glory which lay dormant in an aisle of the church throughout the year, and which was taken out that day, once its gold and silver had been polished, once it had been decorated with flowers, once the colours of the holy plaster figurine had been brightened up with a little pink paint, often the same as that used to preserve the hulls of the boats.

The fishermen themselves would then carry the altar, of biblical weight, and the procession moved slowly and piously through the narrow streets of the town, making its way to the harbour, where the Priest performed his duty by dispersing holy water before setting off at the same slow pace, accompanied by prayers, towards the church, to the sound of the exhausted brass band with its increasingly false notes, due to weariness and all the glasses of wine everyone was offered at each stop.

Once the church was reached and the altars replaced in the shade of their alcove until the following year, the Mass would be said. Not all the crowd could fit into the building and many people remained outside, in the square, where on that day not a single one of the lava paving slabs could be seen.

In the evening, after the Christian ceremony, it was time for the pagan festival. The harbour would be illuminated by paper lanterns which occasionally caught fire and would then fly off into the velvety black air, in glittering shreds, briefly sparkling, among clouds of gold dust that drew them upwards and eventually faded when confronted by the splendour of the stars that gazed down upon them, mocking, eternal and dreamlike.

Large tables would be erected, simple planks on trestles, and everyone brought their own bread, their wine, their olives, their pickled capers, their marzipan fruits, their pork and goats' meat, smoked or dried, their honey cakes filled with cream, their pistachio *entremets* and their *citron* and orange liqueurs. Between the laughter and the sounds from the orchestra made up of a few surviving members of the brass band reinvigorated by shots of marc, people would dance. This continued until dawn.

Nowadays, the fishermen still feel they should attend the Tuna Mass. But there is no longer a procession that precedes it. And no more feasting afterwards. Just a meal with the same fishermen. Still held at the harbour. A large table is sufficient. Just men on their own. The wives don't even come anymore.

Still less the children. They drink more than they eat, and it all ends with serious drunkenness, bouts of migraine-filled stupor and a number of rekindled quarrels. The town council attends the Mass, the Mayor to the fore, who always wonders what on earth he is doing there and champs at the bit. There are also some elderly people present who feel that the hour of reckoning has come and who tell themselves that it may perhaps be wise to sort themselves out. After all, one never knows. It could be useful and it's free.

Since the presbytery in its reduced dimensions resembles a doll's house, the Priest gradually took over the church as it began to be deserted by the congregation. With patience and perseverance, he has made it an annexe of his living quarters, a sort of large warehouse in which he has spent years reconstructing the hull of a ship, which had broken up on the reefs that ring the island, the pieces of which he has patiently gathered together, bit by bit, making countless trips during a long summer and filling carts and wheelbarrows borrowed from people here and there.

The sight of the wrecked ship put together again by inexpert hands is startling because, seeing it like this, huge and damaged, stretching what remains of its broken masts up to the vault, a gigantic, battered mass, dwarfing everything that surrounds it, you wonder whether it is the wreck that has been brought into the church, or whether the church has been built around it in order to preserve this remarkable relic, well and truly a ghost vessel, a ship of the dead, the barque of Osiris and Charon.

A confessional and a dozen or so pews remain, nevertheless, surrounded by piles of cardboard boxes and unused hives on which one can sit in order to hear Mass.

The masses are of unparalleled brevity, and only the Mayor still finds them too long. The Priest did not wait for a new council to adjust the liturgy: after a hurriedly recited Our Father, he passes abruptly to his sermon, which generally only lasts a few minutes and in which, accompanied by the loving flight of a few bees, he gives news of his hives, of the weather report, recalls some memories of his years in the seminary on the mainland, and which he ends by reading out the small ads that have been entrusted to him.

Since his belly no longer allows him to bear the sourness of the wine used at Mass, nor the host which sticks insidiously to his dentures, he decided three years ago to do away with communion, but he does not forget the collection, which he carries out himself, even jotting down in a little notebook what everyone has given, not forgetting to remind certain people of their stinginess at the end of the year. The service ends with a hurried blessing and a prayer to the Virgin, who continues to be the island's great deity of the water, the depths and the winds.

When he had walked into the church, the Mayor had noticed the Teacher, sitting in the back row. He was holding a thick brown envelope under his arm, which the Mayor looked at anxiously. Once the service was over, the Teacher approached him in the square, while the rest of the congregation dispersed and the fishermen returned in groups to the harbour.

"Would you have a few minutes to spare, Mr Mayor? I should like to tell you about my discoveries."

The Mayor had no other choice but to take the Teacher into his office nearby. A syrupy smell of anisette hung in the room, and the Mayor felt so embarrassed when he caught the Teacher looking at the two sticky glasses left on top of the desk and at the empty bottle protruding from the wastepaper basket, that he felt bound to offer an excuse.

"I had a visitor."

"I know," said the Teacher immediately. "A policeman. More precisely, a superintendent. He arrived this morning."

"Who told you?"

The Mayor was astonished. He did not even have the strength to be annoyed.

"Everyone knows. News travels fast here. I don't need to tell you that."

The Secretary. It could only be her. That painted-up bonito. She would hear about this on Monday.

"On the other hand, what people don't know is why this policeman is here. They claim that it's to do with the Thermal Baths project. I don't believe a word of that. As far as I'm concerned, I'm sure that his presence has to do with what occurred on the beach, and with what we did afterwards."

The Teacher had never spoken to the Mayor with such assurance. Even during the secret meeting that took place on the memorable evening of the discovery of the bodies, in the boardroom, or in the fishing warehouse. It was as though his shyness, that of a boy who has grown up too quickly and is ill at ease in his new body, had vanished. He seemed galvanised. His expression reflected both a calm determination and a degree of impudence as well. He clung to his envelope and he seemed to be deriving all his strength from it.

"I have here the conclusions of my experiments. They are damning. During the last few days I have been conducting an examination of the currents which, I have no doubt, you know better than I do. But with perseverance, documents and maps, I believe I have also become fairly competent in this area."

He paused, waiting no doubt for the Mayor to react, but the Mayor was doing his best to breathe calmly and to respect the promise he had just made to himself not to lose his temper. With a nod of his head, he indicated that he was waiting for the Teacher to continue.

"I released some dummies, each of which were the weight of a man, at different points of the route taken by the smugglers, as they are called, though I find the word too romantic for these unspeakable wretches who trade in other human beings. Not one of the dummies washed up on the island's beach. Not one, do you hear me, Mr Mayor? I made the experiment twice over. Not a single one ended up on the beach. What is more, only three of them were found. On the mainland. Someone got in touch to tell me. The others have disappeared, carried further out to sea probably. But today, one dummy turned up. A dummy that I released last Sunday, very far from the usual route. To be more precise, immediately adjoining the Saliva of the Dog. What do you reckon? Who would venture down there, in those dangerous waters, unless it was someone who knew the area? That is to say, someone from these parts, Mr Mayor?"

In the Dog Islands, the Saliva is a collection of reefs that barely protrude above the water, like rocky dots that have been spat out there from the mouth of the animal. They do not appear on the maps, which simply indicate the danger that lurks there, for the largest of these stumps is the size of an olive tree. All the fishermen know them and usually avoid them, but at times they go near them – taking care and remaining on their periphery – for their waters are full of fish, and lobsters abound there.

The Mayor felt himself grow weak, as though an invisible and expert hand had made an incision in one of his veins without his noticing; and when he began to feel dizzy, it meant that so much blood had escaped that it was already too late.

What could he say to this lunatic? How to respond to him? What to suggest? Whether there was any basis to his assumption or not, the Mayor sensed that his disclosure would harm the peace of the island and ruin the Thermal Baths project, for investors would not countenance the glare of such gruesome publicity. The men who were prepared to put considerable sums into the realisation of the complex liked obscurity and discretion above all else. The Mayor only dealt with their lawyers, and he had never been in direct contact with those who possessed the money, but he knew who hid behind the initials and the acronyms of their companies and the pleasant smiles of the lawyers. Those men loathed upsets, unexpected events, journalists, courts. All that interested them was putting an honest and discreet façade to their assets, the source of which remained difficult to trace.

If the Teacher's obsession with revealing what he had just told him, whether it was the truth or wild imagination, matched the aggression he himself had displayed with the Superintendent to fulfil his mission, then, the Mayor thought, the island would suddenly disappear beneath the symbolic lava of a new volcano, one that would be more effective than the dormant Brau which overlooked them.

"The sea eludes all calculations, my dear Teacher," the Mayor replied, his voice calm and reasonable to begin with. "I've nothing but praise for your concern about scientific matters, but you see, for the rest of us who were born here, generations of men and women for whom the sea has been a kindly, if irascible companion for thousands of years, we know that it is unpredictable, unfathomable, irrational and mysterious."

The Teacher raised no objections. He was waiting for him to continue.

"You may be right or you may be wrong. I will not give an opinion one way or the other, for I am wise enough to know that in this area we know nothing, we don't know, and we shall never know. If you release another dummy at the same place, at a different time, in another season, you may find it in Argentina or in Greece. As far as I am concerned, your experiments, on which I imagine you have spent a lot of time and money, prove nothing at all. And then, even if your hypothesis were correct, what would it prove? What is it that you are searching for?"

The Teacher took his time before replying. Perhaps so as to relish what he was about to say, perhaps also because he knew that, having spoken, he would not be able to go back on his words and was slightly anxious. A thick silence hung over the Mayor's office, barely troubled by the hum of a large greenbottle fly that was circling about inside the Superintendent's glass, at the bottom of which there was still a sticky trace of anisette, which it was doing its joyful best to imbibe.

"I simply affirm, with evidence to support what I say, that the men whose bodies we have disposed of – against my advice, may I remind you – fell into the water in the area of the Saliva of the Dog. They either fell into the water or else they were pushed. You know as well as I do that no-one dares to venture around the Saliva of the Dog. All the maps show it as a very dangerous zone. No-one, other than the island's fishermen who are familiar with the area and know how to evade the traps."

The Mayor had placed both his hands flat on the desk. He was not moving. He was no longer breathing. He was staring at the Teacher who, for the first time, was holding his gaze and breathing loudly. It was like a duel, without weapons, but which you suddenly felt was going to end in an irreparable way, in the death of one or the other of them.

"Do you realise what you are insinuating?"

The voice of the Mayor had become icy, like a sudden blast of air through the room, whereas outside, the sun, which was still very high in the sky, was baking the black walls of the houses and roof tiles.

"I am not a man to allege things lightly, Mr Mayor. I may be younger than you. I may not come from these parts, as you constantly like to remind me – and what's more, in the light of events and the way in which you are trying to cover them up, I am beginning to be proud of the fact – but I am a responsible person, who says nothing without being certain, and who, when it's a question of such serious matters, weighs up all the factors before discussing them.

"You asked us not to say anything after that memorable morning. I said nothing. But I can no longer keep quiet. I cannot keep to myself what I know and what I have discovered. I didn't want to act treacherously. I wanted to warn you beforehand: if, by Monday morning, you have not made the first move, I myself shall take the account, a copy of which I am leaving with you, to the Superintendent. In it I have recorded the events that took place on the beach and the way in which you have chosen to deal with them. Secondly, I have reported my experiments there, and the conclusions I have drawn from them. This policeman must now be prepared to make use of information that will allow him to investigate and establish the truth. I cannot remain on an island on which men live who are probably guilty of the worst crimes, and where other men live who prefer not to know or to forget about them so that they can continue to sleep with complete peace of mind."

The Teacher had finished. He placed the envelope on the Mayor's blotter. The spring fastener was now back in place. The Mayor even reckoned he heard the sound of the click inside his skull. An infernal device. This was what this madman had just placed in front of him. In one way or another, it was going to explode. No-one could now prevent that. The Mayor had no intention of letting himself be killed, and if the explosion was now inevitable, as he feared, it was best that it blew to pieces the person who had made it possible.

"Don't forget, Mr Mayor, Monday morning."

The Teacher left the room, closing the door quietly behind him.

The Mayor needed calm. And very curiously he, who was normally so on edge, did feel calm. To such a degree that he even wondered whether he had just died. He put his hand to his heart. It was still beating. He left the palm of his hand on the shirt for a few seconds, so that he could feel the beats that were regular and those that were too close together. He had the impression that there, a few centimetres beneath his flesh, there was a small caged animal.

He glanced at his watch. He had an hour before he was due to attend the meal given by the fishermen at the harbour. As the fishermen's boss and as mayor, he could not escape from it. One hour in which to work out how to put the bomb back in the hands of the lunatic who had conceived it. That particular bomb, or else another one. For after all, what mattered was to prevent the Teacher causing harm. The Mayor felt that if this fanatic were to alert the authorities, nothing would ever be the same on the island, to say nothing of the Thermal Baths project which would become a dead issue and a vanished dream. There was no time to go into niceties about the means. All that mattered was that it should be effective. It was necessary to neutralise him.

The Mayor's eyes fell on the glasses that had contained the anisette. At the bottom of one of them, the strange large fly was now lying on its back, its two wings stuck in the drops of alcohol. It was exposing its purplish, plump belly as it feebly wiggled one of its legs. It was dying. The flickering leg was moving less and less. The Mayor could not stop looking at it. Very soon it stopped moving at all, motionless for ever in a translucent coffin that was much too big for it.

XV

THE MAJORITY OF MEN ARE NOT AWARE OF THEIR DARKER side, which nevertheless everyone possesses. It is often circumstances that reveal it, wars, famines, disasters, revolutions, genocides. So when they contemplate it for the first time, in the secrecy of their conscience, they are appalled and they shudder.

The Mayor was confronted by all of this. He discovered nothing that he had not had a premonition about already. What was the point of lying to oneself? He was no longer a child. He had to face the facts: occasionally it is necessary to pass through darkness in order to observe once more the clarity of the dawning day. But he was not a monster, and neither did he hold all the cards. Did anyone actually hold them?

He remembered his grandfather, who had been sent off to the war in his youth, and who came back with one arm missing and his lungs destroyed. He spent his days sitting on a chair, in the kitchen, by the window. His sole occupation was to gaze at the Brau and to feed the birds with crumbs of bread which he placed on the window ledge. The hungriest or the stupidest birds ended on a skewer and he roasted them in the embers of the fire after he had plucked them and rubbed them with oil and garlic.

The Mayor remembered that the old man used to eat them whole, without cleaning them, cracking their tiny bones in his magnificent and very white teeth.

He had come back from the war wounded, but he had returned. One of the very few in his company. The others were all dead. Rebels. Loudmouths. Anarchists and idealists mostly, whom chance had thrown together and who had risen up in a frenzy against their commanding officers, against the war, against the foolishness of a conflict that had gone on for more than three years and had already caused millions of casualties. The NCOs took a dim view of this. The rebellious soldiers were too numerous to stand trial and be shot. That would have risked sowing the spirit of revolution in other minds. They chose rather to send them to take up an impossible or pointless position. A hill with no strategic significance, on which the enemy's artillery could spew out its volleys of gunfire and bombs without causing the least concern. They would be forced to commit suicide. They chose to make them die so that the war could continue its work of mass death without disruption, the ultimate aim being to reshape the map of the world, the powers and the nations, at the dawn of a new century. Of what importance, comparatively, were the lives of a few hundred men, even if what they said was true, even if what they thought was right?

All this was politics. Politics is dirty. It is not moral. Certain men choose to remain clean, whereas others accept that they must get their hands dirty. Both are needed, even if the former are always respected and the latter come to be loathed. Of course, the island was not the world, and the present situation was not war. But the Mayor was a leader, who was concerned about his community, who took care of it, and who knew that in order to do this his job could lead him along muddy paths and to sacrifice an innocent man.

The notion that began to dawn in the mind of the Mayor would be considered immoral and contemptible by the great majority of people. Were he to do this and should God exist, the Mayor would without any doubt spend eternity in the next world shovelling burning coals, being so thirsty he could die, but never able to die. And if God did not exist, there were still the men. When they learned about what he had done, for everything comes to be known eventually, he would have to endure their horror and their opprobrium, perhaps even their justice. Who therefore would dare to be grateful to him?

And even in the highly unlikely event that it remained secret, he would know. He would have to live with what he had done until the end of his life, looking into the little round mirror in the bathroom every morning as he shaved, the face of a shit who believed he had acted for the best. A shit who would constantly be searching for excuses: it was the officers who gave him his orders, the situation was hopeless, communications had broken down and there was chaos; while he would be aware of his wife behind him, her presence, her smell, a woman who knew nothing about it and who, after she had yawned, would come up to him to give him a kiss on his neck which would cause him to shudder like the blade of an axe.

It is strange to think that people who are linked by the same activity can, at the same time, have feelings that are very different: while the Mayor, who was experiencing a deep disgust for himself and was resigning himself reluctantly to having to assume the role of a henchman, the Teacher, who was dressed in his sporting clothes, was making his way at a rapid and steady pace along the path that wound around the flank of the Brau. He did not appear to be suffering from the extreme heat, nor from his exertion, so stimulated was he by his decision and by what he had done. The feeling of being on the right and fair path literally gave him wings. Never had he run so easily, not knowing that in reality he was on the road to ruin.

As for the Superintendent, he was thinking once more of the scene in the Mayor's office that morning. He liked the impression he had made. He liked to frighten people, to see other people having doubts, losing their self-confidence, using the wrong words, too, or muddling them, no longer able to choose the right ones. That had not been very difficult with the Mayor. He had known tougher customers. And he had left him without telling him everything. He had left him with questions to answer. He had simply presented the Mayor with the documents. Without informing him of the conclusions they allowed one to reach. He had destroyed his peace and tranquillity. He imagined the anxiety he was experiencing. Like a weasel whose dirty fangs gnawed at its prey every second of its life, dismembered it and left it half-eaten and contaminated in order to attack the next victim.

The Superintendent knocked back his glass of wine in a single gulp. He was sitting at a table on the terrace of the café. After his visit to the Mayor, he had intended to walk around the town, but very quickly the feeling that he was making his way through an anthill came over him; the size of the streets, that of the houses, the stifling impression of a labyrinth, everything contributed to the sense that he was making his way underground, but doing so in daylight, amid an oppressive heap of construction materials, each darker than the last: paving stones, pavements, walls, roofs, doors, shutters.

The men and women that he had passed hid their faces when they saw him, lowering their eyes, so that they lost all humanity and began to look like large, alarming insects. He had returned to his room and stretched out on the bed, after having taken from his suitcase a bottle of whisky which he had drunk straight from the bottle.

The anthill had vanished, and with it its occupants. He had thought again about his conversation with the Mayor, and the way in which he had departed from him, without saying a word, without revealing any of his intentions, leaving the councillor to roll his bright eyes over the bundle of photocopies, quitting the room without closing the door.

The Secretary had looked at him in alarm. He had noticed that her throat was speckled with red blotches as a result of the shock. He had given her a big smile. The red had shifted to her cheekbones. He had dozed off with this vision in his mind.

The Café Owner brought him the *plat du jour*. The Superintendent did not ask for any explanations. He would not touch it. He was not hungry. He was never hungry. He was constantly thirsty. He ordered a second bottle of wine.

Opposite him, in the centre of the harbour square, a long table about twenty metres long had been erected. The guests had not yet arrived. A warm wind was rustling the paper tablecloths. Some of the napkins were on the ground. A glass had been knocked over. He thought of the Last Supper. Before it had begun. A subject that no artist had ever thought of depicting.

Someone had laid the plates, the glasses, the cutlery, and had then gone away. A servant? One of the apostles? They were only waiting for Christ and his companions, and Judas, for the final act of the rather mundane tragedy that had occupied the minds of a large part of mankind for two thousand years.

The Superintendent had a weakness for Judas. Judas had been loathed now for such a long time. The Superintendent would have liked to be loathed for just as long. Like Judas. Love fades sooner or later. But not loathing. It lingers, even grows sometimes, and constantly reactivates itself. It is the driving force of the human species. In the long run, the triumph of Judas will endure longer than that of Christ, which can be seen crumbling everywhere. The proofs of love are lacking among men, whereas the signs of treason and evil proliferate. The Superintendent poured himself some more wine. In his mind he drank to Judas.

The fishermen gradually arrived and gathered around the table. They spoke in loud voices, hailing one another and laughing in a dialect the Superintendent did not understand. Some of them made their way towards a warehouse. They came out again carrying small casks, baskets filled with bread, jars, plates of cheese and ham. A mass of food and bottles soon cluttered the tablecloth. It was no longer the Last Supper. You were suddenly walking straight into a painting by a Flemish primitive. An abundance of food, drinks, toothless laughter that split the dazed and sunburned faces, unsteady bodies, mounting drunkenness, stupid features. The crude and the idiotic. Eating and drinking. The omission of death, which, however, when you look carefully, can always be found somewhere in the painting: a skull at the foot of a tree, a branch in the shape of bones, two crows, a scythe placed next to a barn, a bare tree in the midst of ripe wheat fields, worms devouring fruit. And what about here, where was death hiding? Was it he himself who embodied it that day?

For his amusement, the Superintendent looked everywhere for real-life reproductions of paintings he had seen in galleries where he often used to go to relax and think before spending his spare time wandering from bar to bar. One might have taken him for a conventional drunkard, a new type of Sisyphus who would swap his rock for a glass that required emptying but never stopped being refilled for him. But alcohol, which was his most faithful companion, was also the most deceptive, because for a long time now it had forbidden him the slightest drunkenness, and the Superintendent was condemned, in addition to eternal lucidity, nevermore to know what he was looking for.

XVI

ON THE FOLLOWING SUNDAY, VARIOUS SIGNS SUGGESTED that something was about to happen.

There was already, and had been since dawn, an oppressive heat, without any breeze. The air seemed to have solidified around the island, in a dense and gelatinous transparency that here and there distorted the horizon when it did not obliterate it: the island hovered in the midst of nowhere. The Brau gleamed with meringue-like reflections. The bare, black lava that lay on top of the vines and the orchards shimmered as if it had suddenly become liquid again. The houses were very quickly filled with an enervating exhalation that wore out the body and the mind. There was no freshness to be enjoyed there.

Then there was a smell, almost imperceptible to begin with, which you could persuade yourself was something you might have dreamed about, or else that it came from human beings, from their skin, their mouths, their clothing, or from within them. But from one hour to the next the smell asserted itself. It crept in discreetly, almost secretively.

Some people believed that the odour came from the grapes

that had been laid out to dry on the walls. Bunches that include grapes affected by the rain can in their gradual rotting process sometimes secrete this invisible, vaguely sugary mustiness, insipid yet seductive, that carries within it sensuous hints of over-ripe fruit, but also scents of venison, of badly scorched fur on the surface of which a few scraps of meat have been left behind that are starting to rot, and through which tiny white maggots are making their way.

And then, when it is not the grape, the vapours that come from the depths of the earth remain. The island should be imagined as one of many lids set down hurriedly over geological periods on top of the gigantic cauldron that is the planet, filled with burning molasses that never stop bubbling.

The island's memory bears witness to three major eruptions of the Brau over the centuries, and to streams of lava which have almost entirely destroyed the houses every time and killed many people, and yet the survivors have never dreamed of deserting the place. When it is not the volcano's safety valve that opens up, its side slopes periodically release steam and gases, like a pipe-smoker's dreams. That in itself is not the sign of an eruption. This faint stench is reminiscent of a hard-boiled egg that has been cut in half, left on a counter for days, and forgotten.

But what people smelled that Sunday had nothing to do with this. One had to face the facts. It was something very different from insubstantial and purely geological, chemical miasmas. There was something alive about this faint stench. And as the day went on, oppressive and torrid, the air seemed to grow heavy from all this invisible cooking.

The Mayor had not been wrong to say to Swordy that later on, when he thought back to the morning of the discovery of the three corpses, he would tell himself that it had never happened, that it was a nightmare, and gradually, by dint of telling himself that it was a nightmare, the notion would lose its consistency and its distinctness. Eventually, its outlines would lose their clarity. Its faded colours, like those on old Polaroid photos, would make the scene transparent. The bodies of the dead and those of the eyewitnesses would turn into spectres, and then dissolve. There would then be only two or three small steps to take before finally reaching oblivion.

But things did not happen in this way, alas.

The Teacher did not have to come and knock on the Superintendent's door on Monday morning, because on Sunday evening the Superintendent himself, accompanied by the Mayor, came to knock on his door. It was just after eight o'clock and the heat had not yet cooled, any more than the stench of decay had faded, which now wallowed shamelessly in the streets and did its best to get inside the houses.

When the Teacher opened his door and saw the two men, he smiled at the Superintendent and favoured the Mayor with a grateful glance, but when the Superintendent spoke and asked him to confirm his civil status, he stopped smiling immediately and asked what was meant by this.

"You are under arrest."

The Teacher's lips began to quiver and he was unable to control the movement of his eyelashes, which blinked wildly as if their inner mechanism had suddenly malfunctioned. For him it was an enormous farce. The Superintendent and the Mayor, without saying a word, maintained their silence and stared at the Teacher, whose large body seemed to sag and grow weak. There they stood: a man who was astounded facing two others, all three motionless, with the night drooping over their heads.

The previous night, the Superintendent had gone to bed late. Sitting on the terrace of the café and helping himself to more wine the moment the bottle was empty, he had enjoyed the spectacle of the fishermen's dinner. A succinct summing-up of mankind and its decline, or of the very tenets of society. A group like this that clinked glasses and laughed would, a few hours later, start shouting at one another and making acrimonious remarks and threatening gestures. The jokes turned into barbs, the laughter into arrows, the personalities grew menacing. It was not just the glasses brimming with alcohol that were responsible for this. It only happened when the film that had formed over a jar in which tarantulas, woodlice and cockroaches were swarming was removed. It was not he who had created the poison. He was simply releasing it, nothing more.

Blows had been avoided that evening, but it had been a close-run thing. They had all left without saying goodbye to one another, staggering about, leaving their upturned chairs behind them and the banquet table strewn with broken glasses and litter. Only the Mayor had stayed behind, with a fisherman sitting beside him who had a trapeze-shaped head and hair like a bear's fur. The Mayor was whispering in his ear while the other man was sipping glasses of marc, his elbows on the table, and nodding from time to time. When the two men eventually got to their feet, they shook hands at length.

The following day, Sunday, while he was still stretched out on his bed in his pyjamas but awake, there was a knocking at his window. The Superintendent drew back the curtains and recognised the Mayor. Without bothering to get dressed, he opened the door to him and invited him in. The Mayor preferred to remain in the doorway. The Superintendent grabbed hold of a bottle of whisky from the bedside table and knocked back a mouthful with which he gargled as if it were a mouthwash, then swallowed it.

"It's early, Mr Mayor. Too early for me. I'm a creature of the night. I should have warned you."

"I would not have allowed myself to disturb you were the matter not serious."

"A serious matter? You'll get me excited! A serious matter on your island that doesn't exist, that barely exists – I'm curious. Could you enlighten me?"

"The best thing would be for you to come with me to my office. They're waiting for us there."

"Who is?"

"The witnesses."

The Superintendent snatched hold of his clothes which had been thrown in disorderly fashion onto the chair. He started to slip on his boxer shorts.

"Do you know why I do this job? No, you don't know, and you would never guess. I chose it because I wanted to kill. Yes, kill. The funniest thing about this story is that I've killed very few people in my career."

The Superintendent was struggling with a vest that had once been white, but which with wear and tear and countless washes, no doubt badly supervised, had become yellow in places.

"I took the wrong path. Had I chosen violent crime, as was the tradition in my family, I would probably have been more likely to realise my dream. What pleasure I took in gazing into the face of my father, who was a real scoundrel, when I informed him that I wanted to study the history of art and not carry on the business of racketeering and extortion of every kind that had become his speciality. He died shortly afterwards. I hope I was partly responsible for his death."

The Superintendent had slipped on his trousers. He sniffed his socks before putting them on. He put on his shoes and tied the laces. The Mayor gazed down upon his skull and its shiny bald spot. He would have liked to have a brace with which to drill a hole inside it, to see the shape of the Superintendent's brain. Standing in the doorway, he could hear the sea and the cries of the birds. He also detected a strange smell which he attributed to the lack of ventilation in the shop that the Café Owner had converted into a bedroom, and also to the body that had slept there, but perhaps the smell came from outside, without his being able to detect the source.

"Let's go, I'm ready. We mustn't make your witnesses wait. I feel that this Sunday is going to be a fine day."

The Superintendent took care to slip the bottle of whisky into his coat pocket and he followed the Mayor.

The witnesses were waiting at the town hall, sitting on the bench opposite the Secretary's office, empty on this Sabbath day. The Policeman recognised the stout man gazing at the floor as the fisherman the Mayor had been talking to the previous evening. His head was enormous and his wig was indeed made of a synthetic fur, like that used to cover the bodies of teddy bears.

By his side stood a young girl of about ten years old. She was as erect as he was bent. She was staring at the desk in front of her. She had large green eyes, slightly too large, slightly too wide open, within a slim, pale face, such as you find in certain portraits by Lucas Cranach. She had placed her delicate and abnormally long hands in her lap. She was dressed in a full red cotton skirt and a blue checked blouse. On her feet she wore canvas ballet shoes. The tips of her toes barely reached the ground. Her red hair was tied back from her domed forehead in a ponytail. The Superintendent thought she must be extremely serious, a seriousness that could indicate either remarkable intelligence or profound stupidity.

The Mayor pointed to the door of his office. They sat down. But the Superintendent preferred to perch on the corner of the desk, one buttock on the wooden surface, the other hanging free. The young girl sat down on the edge of a chair opposite him.

"I'm listening," said the Superintendent.

The girl looked at the fisherman, but he kept his gaze resolutely fixed on the carpet that covered the lava floor. She then glanced at the Mayor, who was of no more help to her. She turned towards the Superintendent.

"Do you want to say something to me, my dear? What's your name?"

"Mila."

"How old are you?"

"Eleven years old."

"I'm listening to you, Mila."

"It was the Teacher."

"What about the Teacher?"

"He did things."

"Things?"

"He touched me."

"He touched you."

"Yes."

"Where did he touch you?"

The child pointed to the inside of her thighs.

"In that place?" asked the Superintendent. "Is that where the Teacher touched you?"

Mila nodded, fixing her large green eyes on those of the Superintendent, who gazed at her with mounting interest.

"He touched you with his hands?"

"Yes. And his fingers too."

"His fingers?"

"Yes. He stuck his fingers inside."

The Superintendent turned towards the Mayor, who was nervously tearing up a piece of blotting paper. A small heap of pink litter was piling up on his desk pad. He looked up at the Superintendent, who was studying him thoughtfully. The Mayor, embarrassed, could not hold his gaze for long and began to shred his blotting paper once more. The voice of the young girl was heard again.

"He put his thing in as well."

"His thing?"

"The thing that men have. He put it in there as well."

"The Teacher?"

"The Teacher."

At that moment the father was wracked with a violent bout of coughing which shook his chest and jolted his large head. The croaking went on for so long that it was as if he was about to spit out his lungs or suffocate.

"You swear that everything you're telling me is true?" asked the Superintendent, taking the child's face in his hand and forcing her to look at him. "Do you swear? It's very serious, what you're telling me."

"I swear," the young girl replied without hesitation. "It's the truth. I swear."

Then the Superintendent turned his back on her and looked once more at the Mayor, who was tearing up another sheet of blotting paper but keeping his head down. As for the Superintendent's face, it lit up with a big smile, such as one sees on certain paintings of saints or mystics. At that moment he was the image of unbounded happiness. He even forgot about the bottle of whisky in his pocket, which had suddenly become a needless accessory. Even though he was not expecting it, even though he had not come here for this purpose in the slightest, life was providing him with an exhilaration that alcohol had failed to provide for a long time now.

XVII

WHEN THE DOCTOR OPENED HIS DOOR, HE WAS DRESSED in his perennial linen suit, but he had rolled up his trouser legs halfway up his ankles, revealing his large red feet streaked with meandering and swollen veins. Everyone who was at the door was looking at the Doctor's feet, which had left damp patches on the paving stones. And he stared at his visitors, a curious crew if truth be told, consisting of the Mayor, the Superintendent, Furry, a somewhat simple fisherman who had concealed his baldness for many years beneath a filthy patchwork of tatters and fluff, and his daughter Mila, whom he had brought up on his own, his wife having left him for a man from the mainland when the child was barely a few months old.

"We need you," said the Mayor.

Somewhat surprised, the Doctor ushered them into his house with his right hand, in which he held a book. They all went inside. The Mayor led the way into the waiting room.

"Before anything else, the Superintendent and I need to speak to you. Furry can wait here with Mila."

The fisherman and his daughter sat down in the waiting

room. The young girl grabbed a comic from among the magazines and newspapers that cluttered a low table, and her father took up his customary pose, shoulders tipped forward, and his enormous head dragged down towards the floor by its considerable weight, as if it were about to be crushed there.

The Doctor's surgery testified to a sophistication that the Superintendent did not expect to find in this land of primitive people. Lots of books lined the walls, old and rare editions, judging by the elegance of their bindings, which filled bookcases whose design and patina, carved as they were from a wood with reddish tints, perhaps walnut, had been polished to a smooth sheen.

It was the Mayor who summed up the situation. The Superintendent did not interrupt and allowed him to speak. The Doctor listened, fiddling with his moustache which he had not dyed that morning because it was Sunday, and which was glowing in all its grey-haired splendour. Beneath his desk, he was wriggling his toes as though he were trying to play a tune on a piano. His large, smiling face was listening to the Mayor, whose awkwardness at repeating the young girl's comments had not escaped him. When the latter stopped speaking, the Doctor took out a handkerchief from his pocket to mop his brow.

"And you are expecting me to examine her?"

"You have understood correctly, Doctor," the Superintendent said. "It is vital that the assertions this child has made are corroborated by clinical observations. If, as she claims, repeated rapes have actually taken place, this should be visible."

"Of course."

"You don't appear to be surprised by what brings us here. Might you have had your suspicions?"

"Not in the least, But I am no longer very young, and, without having explored everything fully, sufficiently familiar with human nature to know what it is capable of. I am going to ask you to leave the room. Tell the young girl to come in, please."

The Doctor stood up and walked towards a door, which he opened. The Superintendent found himself in the consulting room, with a patient's examination table, some instruments, metal and glass cupboards, a height-measuring rod, a weighing machine, and a washbasin over which the Doctor was already busy soaping his hands vigorously. Then he ran the tap, carefully rinsed his hands, and dried them with a clean paper towel which he then threw into a tall metal bin. When he returned to his office, Mila and her father were standing side by side, waiting.

"Not you, Furry, I need to see your daughter on her own."

The fisherman seemed relieved. He went back to the waiting room and closed the door behind him. The child did not appear to be distressed by the Doctor. She knew him, of course, as did everyone else on the island from having always dealt with him, and from bumping into him in the streets too, but the Doctor was astonished by her calm, given the circumstances, and the absence of any visible emotion. Choosing his words carefully, he explained to her what he was going to do and why he needed to do this. She asked no questions. He told her to lie down on the examination table, to pull up her skirt and to take off her knickers. He put the leg stirrups in place and adjusted their length to the minimum. Without his having to explain to her how they worked, Mila put her feet into them, as if she was used to doing it, and this bothered him. Thighs spread wide, she turned her face to the ceiling of the surgery and closed her eyes. He proceeded with the examination.

XVIII

THE ISLAND HAD NO POLICE STATION, STILL LESS ANY cells. Yet they had to find a place in which to lock up the Teacher. After considering the matter, the Mayor told the Superintendent that beneath the town hall there was a large cellar, virtually empty, that was used as the boiler room. It was sealed by a solid door. A hole equipped with bars, situated just above ground level, let in a feeble light. The Superintendent went to see it. It was perfect. The Mayor had Swordy bring along a mattress, a can of water, a basin and a chamber pot. The gas boiler worked slowly and with a buzzing sound, but it was enough to dry out the natural damp of the place. Swordy did what he was told without asking questions. What he liked above all else was not knowing.

The two men led the Teacher in. He put up no resistance, which surprised the Mayor, who expected him to refuse to follow them, to argue, and to protest his innocence when he found out the crime of which he was accused, which the Superintendent had told him about. On the contrary, he seemed stunned and as if deadened, on the point of bursting into tears like a child caught misbehaving. He took it all calmly. He did not even kiss his wife or his little twin daughters, who had appeared at the doorway after having no doubt heard the reason for his arrest, and who were hugging one another as the three men went on their way.

The Superintendent decided not to arrange the confrontation with the young victim that same day. He knew the benefits that can accrue from a night of silence and solitude in a man who has just been snatched from his peaceful life and put up against the wall. He double-locked the door of the cellar and slipped the key into his coat pocket. He appeared to suddenly discover the presence of a bottle of whisky there, from which he took a large gulp. He offered the bottle to the Mayor, who refused. The two of them went upstairs to the councillor's office.

"I owe you my apologies and gratitude, Mr Mayor," said the Superintendent, whose bald patch seemed even shinier than it had when he woke up. "In coming here, I did not think I would have such a treat to get my teeth into. You must admit I've been lucky!"

"What do you mean?" the Mayor said with restraint.

"I arrive, and a crime takes place."

"Does that surprise you?"

"Not really. My understanding has always been that it is the law that creates the offence, and not the offence that creates the law. It's rather like the chicken and the egg, but more complicated. Do you follow me?"

"I think so."

"If I had never landed on your island, this child might perhaps have continued to put up with what she has endured, in silence, without complaining."

"But you came for something else. The photographs that you showed me."

"Let's leave that aside for the time being, your teacher is much more interesting."

The Superintendent drained his bottle and tossed it in the direction of the Mayor's wastepaper basket. It shattered on the ground.

"Missed! You can't always win. See you tomorrow, Mr Mayor. Sleep well."

And he left the office without even bothering to pick up the broken glass and put it in a dustbin.

The findings made by the Doctor during his examination of the child, and which he had immediately made known to the Mayor and the Superintendent, were beyond doubt. The young girl was no longer a virgin. Her condition indicated that her hymen had been broken for some time and that she must have endured frequent penetration. She had tolerated the examination with complete calm. The Doctor said he was absolutely astonished by this. She had kept her gaze fixed on the ceiling and, when he told her that he had finished, she had removed her feet from the stirrups, put on her knickers and pulled down her skirt. She had sat down on the examination table while the Doctor washed his hands.

"And so it was the Teacher who did that to you?" he had asked as he turned his back to her.

"Yes, Doctor."

"You swear to me?"

"Yes, Doctor."

"When did this begin?"

"A year ago."

"And why didn't you say anything?"

"He threatened me."

"With what?"

"To give me bad marks."

"And had you never had bad marks?"

"No. Never. Only very good ones."

The Superintendent asked the Doctor to write an account of the examination and the conclusions he drew from it. This took him more time than he thought, not that he had any doubts about the examination that he had carried out: the young girl had lost her virginity and it had not taken place the previous day. He was certain of that. No lesion or tearing was visible. Furthermore, the plasticity of her vagina substantiated the fact that she had had intercourse several times, probably regularly. Of that he was also certain. What bothered the Doctor was that the girl had recounted the facts with great calm and did not appear to be in the least traumatised, not even upset. If she had come to have her knee disinfected following a fall in an alleyway, she would not have acted any differently. How could a young girl endure such assaults and not be affected by them? He reckoned that her smooth, unperturbed face was probably a façade, and that beneath it a great deal of commotion had stacked up over her share of the ruins.

How did the Teacher spend his first night in the darkness of the cellar? What could he be thinking about? What was uppermost in his mind? Astonishment? Anger? Disgust? Fury? Fear? Despair?

In the morning the Mayor, who had retained a duplicate of the keys to the door, came and brought him a cup of coffee and a brioche. He found him sitting on the mattress, staring at the wall opposite him. The Mayor put down the coffee and the brioche at his feet. The Teacher turned towards him.

"You know very well that I'm innocent!"

"I only know what the young girl says."

"She's lying!"

"That's what you say."

"You're disgusting! It's you who told her to lie."

"You're in a very tricky situation."

"Come on now, this won't last! It's not possible!"

"If you're sure."

"I just need to be face to face with her, for her to tell the truth. She's a good girl. An excellent pupil."

"We shall see."

"This is all a put-up job! It won't prevent me from giving my report to the Superintendent! You're a shit!"

The Mayor left the cellar and double-locked the door. He heard what sounded like a rising groan from the other side, or perhaps it was sobbing.

XIX

WHEN SOMEONE WANTS TO PUT DOWN HIS DOG, HE accuses it of being mad. The old methods have been tried and tested and function at any time. One only has to adapt them to current tastes. Whether or not the Teacher was innocent of what he was accused of was not the main problem. The main problem was that he was being accused. In a way, and whatever the outcome of the matter, the harm had been done. It would remain and nothing could wash it away.

Had the accusation remained secret, it would have had little impact, but when on Monday morning, after leaving their homes, the children returned a few minutes later saying that the school was closed and that the Teacher was not there, the adults began to wonder what had happened. Some mothers went and knocked on his door. No-one answered. And then the news spread, from whom or from where nobody knew, that the Teacher had raped Furry's little girl.

Then they ran over to Furry's house, a number of them this time, panic-stricken mothers clasping their children to their sides. When Mila came out of the front door, looking, some said, like a young nun or a saint, upright and calm, noble and remote, she confirmed the rumour in a voice devoid of any anger. Yes, the Teacher had forced himself on her with his thing. The girl added nothing else. She went back inside. People were dumbfounded. Then there were shouts. A growing crowd of mothers, and men too, who had been alerted by the din and were being told the news.

All this ambulant fury was directed once more at the Teacher's house. They yelled. They shouted out insults. They insisted on seeing him come outside for they did not yet know that he was in the cellar of the town hall. They threw stones at his windows. They shattered the panes. They slashed the wooden door with kicks and knives. They scribbled insults on the walls. They grew slightly breathless, since no-one appeared at the windows. They came to the conclusion that the house must be empty.

The women went away with their children. The men ran off to inform the other men. In less than an hour the entire island was distilling the news as though it were a rare and heady spirit. Intoxicated by it, no-one took any notice of the foul stench that had grown steadily worse. It seemed to be flowing down the sides of the Brau like invisible and volatile lava. It invaded the smallest alleyway, it had found its way into the gaps in the walls and the roofs and invited itself inside the houses, inspected them room by room and made itself at home like a shameless hotel guest who is getting ready to spend a long and well-fed stay with his embarrassed hosts.

On her walk back from the beach, the Old Woman passed by the Teacher's house shortly after the horde of mothers had left. America, whom she had met along the way, had told her everything about Furry's little girl. She read the words of hatred, even dipped her fingers in the paint that had not yet dried and was still dripping. With the tip of her foot, she pushed aside some glass shards. Her cold eyes smiled and she spat on the ground.

The sky, neither blue nor grey in this late September weather, but covered in a smoky glaze, transformed the sun into a doughy, uneven mass, spreading over it like rancid butter and blurring its contours. The sea-birds, gulls, terns, eagles, kittiwakes, albatrosses and oystercatchers, were flying in a strange manner, concentrically – not so much above the waves and close to the shore as they normally did, or close to the boats on the quay, excited by the smell of fish that never leaves the nets completely, but around the slopes of the Brau, in a noisy, shrill, circular flight, eventually constructing a sort of ring of wings, feathers, beaks and cries, bringing the dead volcano back to life in what to us is a meaningless circular existence.

And then there was the stench. Which no longer had anything pleasant or indeterminate about it: it was a smell of decay that was settling over the island. A smell that was unmistakeable, like one that comes from a thicket when a wounded animal goes to die there and its corpse decomposes over time, loses its original shape, attracts flies, worms and maggots, swells up with gas, grows huge, decomposes, bursts and releases all its foul fluids which trickle away in blackish streams.

It was hard not to think of the bodies of the drowned men within the bowels of the Brau. It was impossible that three corpses buried dozens, perhaps even hundreds of metres inside the earth should manage to saturate the air of the entire island with their miasma, but the stinking air seemed to express their presence, their anger and their bitterness. This foul smell was the first act in a vengeance that would unravel at an implacable tempo: the dead would make the living pay for their indifference. They had treated the bodies of their fellow human beings as they would the remains of animals. They had chosen silence rather than words. They would be punished for this.

The Superintendent did not hurry to arrange the confrontation. It took place midway through Monday afternoon, in the stifling atmosphere of the council room. They had drawn the curtains, both to conceal themselves from the crowd in the town square that had grown steadily larger, and to protect themselves from the sun, which seemed to want to bring the island and its inhabitants to boiling point.

The Mayor had already been in his seat for an hour, as had the Doctor, whom he had asked to come slightly earlier. The Superintendent entered, dressed as though he were going to a wedding, wearing a blue suit with thin white stripes, a beige silk shirt, a red tie and polished shoes. He had brushed back his sparse hair with a shiny lotion. Freshly shaved, his greenish complexion was now exposed; it did him no favours and provided evidence of his poor health. However, there was no bottle to ruin the shape of any of his pockets.

"Here we are, gentlemen. Time's up!"

"Would you like me to leave?" asked the Doctor, who was wiping his neck with his large, dirty scented handkerchief.

"Do no such thing," replied the Superintendent, who was examining everything in the room as he walked around it. "The more the merrier!"

Then turning suddenly towards the two men, he exclaimed with a look of excitement in his eye:

"Have you seen them outside? The noose is tightening! I like crowds when they are full of electricity. They become unpredictable! Anything can then happen. Come and take a look at them: monsters in the pit waiting for their meat to be distributed. None of them wants to miss it and each of them hopes to bring back its share. It's wonderful."

He had just drawn back the curtain of one of the windows that overlooked the square. The Mayor had got to his feet reluctantly, and the Doctor had followed him, both because he did not want to leave him on his own and also so as not to upset the Superintendent, whose nervous and no doubt unbalanced temperament he had seen through. All three of them found themselves gazing at the square.

"So, what do you reckon? We're at the theatre, are we not?"

The Mayor could not conceal his surprise. The Doctor disguised his beneath his smile, but the way in which he vigorously wiped his forehead proved that he was concerned. There, below them, taking up the entire gloomy perimeter of the square, were hundreds of women, children and men huddled together, a compact mass that was buzzing like a beehive. Hypnotic, the music of their voices sounded like a litany, entrancing, nasal, basic, generous and all-enveloping, and it reached the ears with a buzz that made every part of the body quiver, and eventually rose to the brain to irritate it.

Suddenly, without anyone knowing why, the layer of sound subsided, then stopped, while at the same time, at the far end of the square, opposite the town hall, towards the alleyway that bordered the southern corner of the church, a ripple ran through the crowd which separated and divided in two, as though it had been sliced with the blade of a scalpel. Then, in the narrow opening that gradually split in two, the Mayor, the Doctor and the Superintendent saw the slim figure of Mila appear, all dressed in white, and holding a large candle in her joined hands.

Why a candle, and who had given her the idea?

The fact remains that the candle and the clothing produced their effect. The crowd grew silent. Motionless, they gazed at the girl, who was followed by her father, Furry, who was not carrying a candle but also had his hands joined, and was staggering slightly – drunk perhaps, drunk in all probability, as was his custom – with his lopsided bearskin wig on his head.

As the girl passed by, the men removed their hats and the women crossed themselves, some of them even knelt down. All this without anyone conferring with anybody else. All this a result of drawing on the old resources, still active, of fears and sacred signs that are denied, that are disregarded, but which linger on and raise their ancient heads when it is necessary, when people are powerless, when they don't know what to do, when they are at their wits' end.

The girl moved forward, slowly, gazing straight ahead of her, dignified and serious, looking only into the distance, unconcerned about the crowd surrounding her, holding her candle as though it were the body of Christ Himself. She walked into the town hall. She disappeared inside, Furry too. The door closed behind them. The crowd remained silent.

"Splendid, no?" exclaimed the Superintendent. "At last, we know how to have fun in your dump!"

XX

A FEW SECONDS LATER, THE GIRL AND HER FATHER ushered in with them a scent of warm wax and whiffs of marc. Mila was holding her candle in one hand now and had blown it out. The Mayor drew the curtains and pointed to the chairs. The girl sat down. Furry beside her, yawning and adjusting his wig. The Superintendent took control of matters.

"Within a few moments, the Teacher will come into this room. I shall have him sit down here, opposite you. He will be far enough away not to do you any harm, but close enough for you to be able to see him clearly, and for him to see you. I shall sit here. There are enough of us to protect you from him, so you have nothing to fear. I shall put questions to you, shall ask you to respond to them, to describe what happened as you have done already. The Teacher may shout, lose his temper, threaten you and plead with you. You should take no notice of what he does or says. You should only concern yourself with the truth. Do you understand?"

"Yes. The truth. I understand."

"Good. Mr Mayor, would you be so kind as to go and fetch the accused?"

The Mayor appeared disconcerted. Perhaps he was expecting the Superintendent to take responsibility for collecting the Teacher from his improvised prison? He gave the Doctor an imploring look, which the Superintendent noticed and understood.

"Have someone go with you, if that would reassure you."

Never had the journey from the council room to the cellar seemed as long to the two men. The building, which was just like all the other constructions on the island, may have had dwarf-like proportions, but that day the Mayor and the Doctor had the impression that the space was expanding, that the corridors were becoming longer as though they were made of a pliable and soft material, that the staircases were increasing their steps and never stopped going down, and that the cellar in which the Teacher was imprisoned was situated at the centre of the earth, in the place where everything is born and everything dies, where all the opposing forces rise up and destroy one another.

The Mayor took the key out of his pocket, paused for a moment and looked at the Doctor who, his face gleaming with sweat, favoured him with his impassive smile.

The Teacher was lying down on the mattress, in a position that made one think of statues in cathedrals. You might have thought he was dead. The Doctor saw immediately that he was breathing and reassured the Mayor with a wave of his hand. The Teacher drew himself up onto his elbows. He looked at them. A smile of deep sadness appeared on his lips.

"Even you, Doctor! Are you not ashamed . . . ?"

The Doctor's smile faltered a little but it did not disappear.

"You are going to be confronted by the young girl," said the Mayor straight away. "Kindly follow us."

"Yes. Let's get it over with."

He got to his feet with difficulty. The night spent in this inhospitable place devoid of all comfort had made him move like an old man. He brushed against the Mayor and the Doctor without even looking at them. The Doctor noted that an acrid smell of congealed sweat arose from his body, one that can be detected in hospital rooms in the morning, hovering over the beds of those with high temperatures who have spent the night tossing and turning in their damp sheets.

The Teacher smiled at Mila as he entered the room, and greeted her father and called him by his name, but Furry did not answer. He also said hello to the Inspector. It was not yet a defeated man who was taking his place in the council room, but a shocked and weakened human being, and one who, in spite of everything, was confident in the outcome of the confrontation and the truth it would enable to be brought to light.

The Superintendent bowed his head, Furry lowered his, and the girl greeted the Teacher by addressing him as "Sir", which seemed to please him. He took this as proof of respect, a respect that could not exist if the facts that the girl had accused him of had been genuine. But apart from him, for anyone else who heard this word uttered by the child and the way in which she had pronounced it, the effect it produced could be a chilly one, because one could fancy that it suggested the influence and limitless authority the Teacher exerted over the girl, and which had possibly enabled him to demand the worst from her, and to obtain it.

So, how to summarise what followed next? The Teacher destroyed himself, without anyone having the least need to help him die: he managed it so very well on his own. And as he lost his footing, as he felt the situation developing into a perfectly constructed trap for him and one that would leave him without any hope, his voice grew increasingly weaker, shakier and emptier, and the more he moaned.

The child's performance was perfect in every respect. When the Superintendent asked her to describe how all this came about, she adapted her manner, like the good pupil she was, speaking in her sweet, birdlike voice. She began by saying that the Teacher often congratulated her for her excellent results. In front of the whole class, he praised her conscientiousness and her ability, saying that she was a role model, a gifted child, a little treasure, adding that furthermore she was polite, had good manners, and was so charming and very pretty.

The Superintendent paused to turn towards the Teacher so that he could ask him whether all this was true, whether these were his words. He confirmed that this was the case.

"And do you often speak about a pupil like this in front of the whole class?"

The Teacher replied that no, he did not do so frequently, but that in this case he had wanted to encourage the girl, who had obvious gifts, who did not come from a milieu that could help her, and that she deserved praise all the more for it.

"What are you trying to say about her family background?" asked the Superintendent.

Attention turned towards Furry, who did not react. Perhaps he did not realise that they were talking about him. He gazed at the table with an idiotic expression. With his wig and his large animal-like eyes, you would have thought he had escaped from a zoo.

"I know that she lives alone with her father, who is often

away on his boat. She does not have the usual life of a child of her age. She has no support. I wanted to be kind."

"Kind?" the Superintendent repeated as he loosened the knot of his tie which, being too tight, had left a red mark on his yellow throat as though someone had been trying to strangle him.

The Teacher did not say anything in reply. The Superintendent told the child she could continue.

"Sometimes, when the Teacher passed along the rows, he stopped beside me. He looked at what I was writing. He bent down and came very close to me. I could smell his breath and his aroma. The heat of his body too. He was really close. I didn't dare to continue. I was frightened that I would write something stupid, right there, in front of him, and that he would notice it. But he said nothing. He stopped for a moment, and sometimes he would stroke my hair, or put his hand on my shoulder. Then I was even more petrified."

"So he touched you."

"Yes. He touched me."

"What do you say about this, Teacher? Is it the truth?"

It was clear that great waves of conscience were swirling around inside the Teacher's head, filling his facial features with sudden and confused stress, with little flickers of irritation, rather like nervous ticks. He was no longer thirty years old. He was of no age. Gradually, he was taking on the appearance of a victim.

"I behaved like that with Mila, just as I did with other pupils."

"With others?"

"Yes. Is it forbidden?"

"To stroke children?"

"You call it 'stroking' and immediately give the word a

perverse connotation. They were simply gestures of sympathy, of encouragement. A way of rewarding them. We are not machines and we are not working with machines."

"And you, my dear," said the Superintendent, "how did you feel when the Teacher touched you like that?"

The child replied immediately, with a quickness that surprised the Superintendent.

"It embarrassed me. I felt ashamed. I felt very uncomfortable, but I didn't dare say so."

"Continue."

"One evening, he asked me to stay on after class. The others left but I didn't. We had taken a very important test the day before and I wasn't sure I'd passed. I was worried. The Teacher spoke to me about the test and about the marks I had got since the beginning of the year. He repeated that he was proud of me, that I was a very good pupil and that I could go to university, which would enable me to get a good job and to leave the island. And he spoke to me about the test."

The girl stopped speaking. She suddenly seemed confused and very emotional. She glanced over at her father, but he continued not to be there. She turned to the Mayor, who looked away, then at the Doctor, who began to inspect his pockets as though he urgently had to find something vital in them. The Superintendent noticed the awkwardness that had just surfaced. He asked the Teacher whether what the child said was true, concerning her studies, her results, and the fact that he had detained her when the others had already left.

"It's true."

"And that doesn't bother you, being alone with a young girl in the classroom, without any witness."

"I never thought of doing anything wrong."

"You're a noble soul, dear Teacher. You live in another world. In a way, you're lucky. Please, Mila, continue," said the Superintendent, with a kindness that he had not shown hitherto.

The girl remained silent. Her eyes shone a little more brightly. The room suddenly seemed to grow smaller. There was no air. The heat created large damp patches beneath everyone's armpits. The Doctor kept mopping his brow. The heavy curtains blocking the windows gave the impression that one would never be able to get out of the place and that one would suffocate there. A tear appeared in the child's eyes, then another. She began to weep, silently, without moving, still upright and with a fixed expression in her eyes.

"Would you like us to stop for a while?" asked the Superintendent.

She shook her head and, through her tears, looked at the Teacher, who appeared shocked.

"That evening, the Teacher told me that I had failed my test."

"But that's untrue!"

"Be quiet! Let her speak!"

"That I would get a bad mark, but that there was perhaps a way for me to get a good mark."

"Why are you lying, Mila? Why are you talking nonsense?"

The Teacher had got up from his seat and was leaning over towards the girl, who appeared frightened.

"Sit down at once or else I shall have you tied to the chair! Is that what you want? Sit down!"

The Superintendent had to wait for a few seconds before the Teacher obeyed him. He collapsed onto the chair like a bundle of washing.

"Please, go on."

"The Teacher made me come and see him, in his office. He stroked my hair and my cheeks. He told me that it didn't matter having a bad mark occasionally, that I was a very good pupil, and that it was a mishap. He made me sit on his lap."

"BUT THAT'S NOT TRUE! YOU'RE LYING!"

"I didn't want to. He forced me to sit down. He continued speaking to me as he stroked me. He put his hand on my thighs."

"SHE'S LYING!"

"He told me that I was beautiful, that I should be nice. He pulled up my skirt. He fondled my knickers."

"STOP IT! WHY ARE YOU SAYING THIS?"

"I could no longer move. I thought I was dead. He put his fingers inside my knickers. He stroked me there, in the place you know. He took my other hand. He slipped it inside his trousers. I felt his thing which was hard."

"THIS IS UNBEARABLE! WHY ARE YOU LYING, MILA?"

"He forced me to fondle it. He talked to me about the good mark that would replace the bad one. In the evening when I got home, I vomited. I had a temperature. I didn't want to go back to school anymore."

The girl stopped speaking. The Teacher was speechless, gazing at everyone with a crazed expression. All of a sudden, as though it came from the depths, a roaring sound arose from within the walls, which were shaking, giving the meeting room the consistency of a marshmallow, while beneath their feet everybody felt the seismic wave that was twisting and turning like a huge snake, thrashing about for all eternity beneath the prong of the trident that was trying to spear it. There were crackling sounds, rattling, scraping noises. Even the big table seemed to be wanting to escape and to be groaning. The Brau was roaring. As though the volcano itself was taking offence at the child's remarks. Only the Superintendent was concerned by the phenomenon, which was something to which he was unaccustomed.

"It's nothing. It's the volcano," said the Mayor, who was not displeased by this diversion.

Calm was restored. The walls regained their impassivity, the big table its silent immobility. The Teacher's torment could continue.

"And what was your mark for this test?" asked the Superintendent.

"The top mark," replied the child, wiping away the large tears that were still flowing down her cheeks with the back of her hands.

XXI

IN THE MINUTES THAT FOLLOWED, IN THE THICK silence of those minutes, there were images. That of the scene which the child had just described, and that of the scene as it must have occurred, and which she was not asked to describe. Her final remark encompassed an entire world simmering with horror and despicable behaviour. The remark became the receptacle for ignominious and contemptible acts which everyone now saw in their imagination as though on a cinema screen, with astonishing clarity. There was no need to add anything else.

The Teacher could no longer hold back his tears. Huddled over his chair, he wept. And throughout the rest of the confrontation, he never once interrupted. Even when the Superintendent gave him the floor, questioned him, asked him to confirm or contradict what Mila had just said about their frequent encounters, about the way in which he had raped her, the whereabouts, the circumstances and the manner in which it had happened, he persisted in maintaining his silence. He continued to weep, sometimes staring at the child, who did not appear to be embarrassed by this, who retained her tear-stained expression most of the time and churned out her relentless story while continuing to weep herself, even though her tears never affected the clarity of her voice.

"Like a sort of trance," the Doctor said later to the Old Woman, who had knocked at his door to have the scene described to her. "The girl behaved as though she was possessed. Something or someone seemed to be talking through her. I am tragically materialistic myself, and don't believe in any form of transcendence, but it was unsettling. Furthermore, one felt that by saying what she had to say she was draining herself of all her strength, and that she was about to faint at any moment."

The Old Woman said nothing. The Doctor had offered her a small glass of liqueur which she had not touched. He was mauling a cigar. She was weighing up everything he had just told her. Dusk had fallen and the crowd that had filled the town hall square for so long had deserted the streets. The Doctor's house stank like a dead dog. Beneath every window he had placed damp clothing to prevent the foul air outside from penetrating the rooms, but it was a lost cause. He frequently raised his handkerchief to his nose while he was with the Old Woman. The bergamot scent with which he had soaked the clothes had not managed to get rid of the stench entirely.

"What's the matter with you? A cold?"

"No. Can't you smell anything?"

"Smell what?"

"That smell that's been around for two days, like a decomposing corpse, everywhere, all over the town."

She looked at him contemptuously as she lightly shook her scrawny head in which her white eyes formed two little bottomless cavities.

When the girl had finished reeling off her evidence, the Superintendent stood up, Furry appeared to wake up, and the Mayor – who could not bear it anymore, and for whom the confined space and the child's account were like having a large hand put over his mouth and his nose, preventing him from breathing – walked over to a window, started to draw open the curtains and grabbed the handle to open a shutter, but then he caught sight of the crowd which he had forgotten all about. He stood stock-still, amazed. Hundreds of eyes were looking up at him. He closed the curtains. A murmur rose up from outside. You would have thought that a gigantic boiler had just been lit.

It was decided that the child and her father should be allowed to leave. Mila picked up her candle again and left the room, her gaze lowered. Furry looked at the Mayor and seemed to be waiting for an instruction. The Mayor looked irritated and signalled for him to go. When the door of the town hall opened and the girl appeared, the hubbub died down, just as it had when she had arrived in the square a few hours earlier. People made way for her once more. She walked, upright and dignified, her extinguished candle in her hand. Her father following behind her looked like a mangy old dog.

People watched her go by. In spite of the heatwave, seeing her look so thin and so pale, each footstep so feeble, made one feel cold all of a sudden, and when she had already crossed half the square and thus found herself in the very middle of the crowd, at the precise intersection of two diagonals that singled her out as the centre of everything, she stopped suddenly, and put her hand to her chest, to her throat, and those who were nearest to her saw her pale eyelids flutter, her eyes roll upwards, and like a *fleur de lin* scythed down by the sharp blade of a sickle she suddenly collapsed, a white corolla on the black paving.

Then a cry burst out from the crowd, a sort of loud, malevolent spitting sound, as shrill as a nail and as cutting as a razor, a cry that embodied a vengeance that demanded to be implemented, and the cry tore through the square, hammered against the fronts of the buildings, knocked on the door of the church, which remained impassive, and finally crashed against the windows of the town hall behind which the Mayor, the Superintendent and the Doctor, all standing, received it like a slap in the face, whereas the Teacher, still seated, seemed to understand that now, as far as he was concerned, whatever happened, whatever he might say or do, all was lost.

XXII

AFTER THE CONFRONTATION, ALL THE TEACHER COULD do was to die. In one way or another. No-one said this, but everyone felt it.

When Mila fainted she was carried home, like a holy relic, held high, and the people started to cross themselves again and to intone prayers. Furry followed behind, in tears. The child was put to bed. Some women soothed her, cooled her down with damp cloths, made her some clear broth and watched over her, while in the kitchen Furry wiped his hand over his fake brown nylon hair, still whimpering and knocking back the glasses which some fishermen came to refill for him, so that he could relate the scene at the town hall to them.

Without anyone having said anything, the square remained filled. Not by the entire crowd, but by a hundred or so men and women, as if in continuous rotation, like vigils that seem to occur without any clear instructions being given. They stared up at the illuminated window of the town hall. They were waiting for the man who had already been stripped of his job, and who they only referred to now as the Monster, to emerge. They were waiting for him to come out, or else they were there to prevent him coming out, which amounted to the same thing.

The other witnesses close to the scene, the Superintendent, the Mayor and the Doctor, were a few steps ahead. They knew that History is full of blind mobs demanding blood. And even though a mob is often wrong, it always ends up by getting what it wants.

The Teacher asked to speak to the Superintendent in private. The Mayor and the Doctor were glad to leave the room, for it was becoming difficult to breathe. They did not reckon it wise to leave the building for the time being. They would have to speak to the crowd. Tell them. Respond. It was not yet time to do so. They shut themselves away in the Mayor's office.

"What do you think he's going to say to him?" asked the Doctor.

"I couldn't give a damn. He can tell him about everything. The three drowned men, what we have done with them, his experiences, his conclusions. The Superintendent will listen to him, but he'll do nothing about it. He's got so many better things now to get his teeth into."

"I'd like to be as certain about that as you are."

"Normally I'm the one who gets anxious and you're the one who puts my mind at ease."

"Times are changing. I don't like what we're doing."

"What do you mean? Neither do I, but it had to be done. Anyway, don't worry yourself. What matters is that he should go away, far from us. That's all. Tomorrow the girl will go back on what she said. He'll be cleared. You'll say that your medical report was misinterpreted. That you're not sure about anything. That you're neither a forensics expert nor a gynaecologist. But all this commotion will drive him off to the mainland far more effectively than any favourable wind. We shall be rid of him. And we shall be able to think about the real problems at last."

The Superintendent had called for three bottles of wine to be brought, and a brandy. The Café Owner served them himself. They watched him as he walked through the square. He carried them carefully and solemnly, as though he had been entrusted with an important mission or was carrying gold. The Superintendent did not allow him to enter the room and made him put everything down at the entrance. He left without having seen the Teacher, of whom he nevertheless provided a detailed description the moment he was outside.

"I wouldn't have recognised him. All those perverse tendencies now show on his face. To think that we entrusted our children to him! Every morning I used to say hello to him innocently, when he set off running. The scum! You should have seen him, sitting on his chair, with his bloodshot eyes, his mouth drooping, and his hands, his fingers, his disgusting big hands on the table in front of him. He's incredibly ugly! If the Superintendent hadn't been there, I wouldn't have been able to control myself, I would have smashed the bastard's face in!"

The Superintendent poured wine into the two glasses. He put one down in front of the Teacher, who had not moved, and knocked back his own in a single gulp. He took off his tie, which he tossed onto the table with a weary gesture, removed his jacket, and unbuttoned and rolled up his shirtsleeves. He came and sat down next to the Teacher, one buttock on the table, the other unsupported, as he loved to do. He poured himself another glass of wine, which he sipped in small gulps while he fixed his gaze on the Teacher. It was as though he was sorrowfully observing a sick animal. The Teacher took a long breath and began to speak:

"There are things I need to tell you about."

"The girl must be clever, to invent such stories," said the Superintendent in a very light-hearted manner.

The Teacher looked at him as though he were suddenly seeing an apparition.

"Sorry?"

"I was telling you that this little girl has plenty of imagination. But you know that, don't you?"

The Teacher opened his mouth wide. He looked flabbergasted. The tide was turning. The Superintendent drained his glass and poured himself another.

"How hot it is! How can you live in this country? Don't you drink?"

The Teacher shook his head. He was unable to speak. So many contradictory thoughts must have been whirling around his mind. And then the bad night, the emotion, the young girl's words, everything had exhausted him. And now these words of the Superintendent, which he wasn't sure he understood properly.

"You're wrong not to. Apart from wine and alcohol, I wonder if there's anything else that deserves to be well known and popular during one's life, for men in any case. We've just had yet another example of their wretchedness."

"So you don't believe everything she's telling you? You believe me? You believe me, don't you, when I say that I'm innocent and that I've done nothing?" said the Teacher in a shaky voice.

The Superintendent looked at the poor wretch for a few seconds. He would not have liked to be in his shoes. He shrugged and stood up. Glass in hand, he walked to one of the three windows. He drew back a curtain and pointed outside.

"Whether I believe you or not is of no importance, and the fact that you're innocent is irrelevant. What matters is what all those people down below, believe. They're like hyenas in a bear pit. Do you like zoos? I can't stand them. I was taken to one when I was a child. A shabby place with grimy trees, and copses filled with rubbish and litter. A smell of shit everywhere, of blood-soaked wounds, and dying animals. Like those there, waiting."

"But you could tell them, explain to them!"

"Explain what to them? That the girl was raped? The Doctor's examination proves it, unless he himself was lying, which after all cannot be ruled out. There's no shortage of scoundrels on this island. That she was lying when she singled you out? That she was reading from a text? That it was probably her degenerate father who raped her, or an uncle, or a cousin, just as retarded as him? That you were here for no reason? That she was acting? That she had been taught a lesson? That pressure had been put upon her? That they had threatened her with sending her father to prison if she did not reel off her story, or that she had been offered money, or I don't know what else? Who would believe me?"

"And yet that is the truth!"

"But who is interested in the truth, my dear Teacher? No-one could care a damn about the truth! What they want is your head, and you know why they want your head: because by arresting you, by bringing you here, by confronting you with the girl, it's as though they have already promised your fine, well-endowed head to all these numbskulls. Imagine their disappointment, if it is taken away from them! Have you ever tried to take away a bone from a dog who was contentedly gnawing at it?"

The Teacher, who, a few seconds earlier, had begun to hope again, now rolled his eyes, incredulous. He appeared to be suffocating. The Superintendent came back and sat down beside him, on the table. He grabbed the bottle of wine.

"And what's more, if you're the rapist then that suits them because you're not like them. You come from somewhere else. You're different. You're a stranger to their island! If I were to tell them that the man who raped the little girl is one of them, that he is just like them, that he comes from the same background as them, from the same mould, is made in their image, do you think they would like or accept the notion? Do you think a human being likes to be shown their own ugliness in a mirror? We never see ourselves as we are, and when it is revealed to us, it's unbearable! Telling them that it's one of their own, a pure local product, a son of the island who touches and penetrates young girls of eleven years old, do you think that's a nice idea? Do you think they would accept the notion? No, you're extremely useful to them, my dear Teacher. They're not going to let you go."

Panic overcame the Teacher. It crept over him rapidly. All his limbs were shaking. He tried to swallow but was unable to do so. He grimaced, gulped the air for breath. The Superintendent handed him the glass of wine once more.

"Drink."

The Teacher obeyed.

"They're sacrificing me. I know things that they don't wish to be divulged. I wrote a report. I was a witness. I've carried out experiments. All that matters to them is their peace and quiet.

The Thermal Baths project, for instance. I can tell you everything. I was there. I understood. They know that I know. That I've guessed. The boats. The traffic. The Mayor. The Doctor. The Old Woman. Swordy. America. All of them. I was with them on the beach. And the Priest too. Later on. In this very place. And then in the cold storage room. They had put the bodies in there. With the fish. Underneath the blue tarpaulin. And then afterwards, the hole in the volcano. They were shoved in there. Then nothing more. Silence. And then afterwards you came along!"

The Superintendent had great difficulty in stopping the Teacher's outburst.

"Do you realise that you're talking like a lunatic? I don't understand a thing you're trying to tell me. Calm down. Is there any point in you getting carried away? It's too late. Too late, as I told you. You don't have the knack. And in any case there's nothing I can do for you."

"But you're a policeman!"

"There again you're wrong."

"What are you talking about?"

"I'm telling you that you're wrong."

"You're not a superintendent?"

"Everyone wanted me to be one. It's my own fault of course: I accepted the role because it made it easier to do what I came to do here, but I'm as much a policeman as you're a cabaret dancer. I'm playing the game. That's all. When I was young, I did a bit of acting at university. They said I was talented. Everyone here wanted to see me as a police officer. I wasn't going to disappoint them. I shoved a card I'd picked up one day from a dead man under the Mayor's nose. He was satisfied with it. I believe it suited him! Everybody lies. Life is a farce. The scene just now amused me a great deal, all that palaver, the little girl who had learned her part, all that damn nonsense paraded like that, shamelessly, but I'm not here for that and I haven't got much time. You're going to have to get along without me."

XXIII

THE STRANGE THING IS THAT THE SUPERINTENDENT called at the Doctor's house that same evening. The Doctor had just come home when there was a knock at the door. He was not expecting to see the Superintendent at his house. He invited him in and asked him why he had come to see him. Why him, rather than the Mayor, who had been the person he had spoken to up till then?

"Why should it matter to you? I'm here, that's all. I'm looking for someone who is prepared to listen to me. Someone who will know how to pass on what I am going to tell them. Your Mayor is too highly strung. He gets angry and he retreats into his anger, but I'm not telling you anything new, you know him better than I do. I enjoyed pushing him to the edge and alarming him, but I soon tired of it. I like playing like a cat with mice, but not for long. And furthermore, with him I would be worried that he might not fully understand what I say to him. Are we going to remain standing in your corridor for ever? It's been a long day."

The Doctor showed him to the door of his study, which was open. He went in and flopped down into the armchair.

"I may not look very serious, but it's a serious matter that brings me to your island. Those who sent me loathe jokes. They loathe many other things, except work that's well done. And it so happens that people have tried to sabotage their work, to impede it, and perhaps even to steal it from them. But I'll explain everything to you. I've had the opportunity to observe you. You're a calm person. You don't appear to be stupid, even though you have dirty hands like the others. You're a run-of-the-mill bastard yourself. I'm not judging you. I'm one too. And of the worst sort. You're a lamb compared to me, but a lamb with a tarnished coat. Are you feeling ill? Why do you keep that handkerchief under your nose?"

The Superintendent did not appear to detect the foul stench of decaying carcass which did not disappear but, on the contrary, grew worse as time went by.

"I get the feeling that you are all going mad. Unless you went mad a long time ago, going round and round in your enclosed world, which would not surprise me. It's high time I left and never come back here again. Would you have something to drink, if it's not too much to ask? And then if you happen to have another of those cigars that you're smoking, I wouldn't say no. I've always thought that smoking those kinds of things helps deep thoughts to surface."

The Doctor went to look for the bottle of *citron* liqueur, two small glasses and the box of cigars. He filled the glasses while the Superintendent was inspecting the box, sniffing certain cigars, and testing their shape between his thumb and index finger. He eventually chose a Robusto, which he cut gracefully before lighting it, taking his time doing so and rolling the cigar so that the ash was uniform. He inhaled the first puffs, chomped the smoke, watching it emerge from his mouth and settle in greyish layers. He seemed satisfied and raised the glass of liqueur to his lips, knocking it back in a single gulp. He made a face as he put it down again.

"How disgusting! Did you make this muck? There should be laws against it."

Which did not prevent him from helping himself to more without asking.

"You imagined a strange sort of chess match. You thought that you could win the game, but there was a snag and you panicked. I don't know who it was who decided to sacrifice a piece, the wretched Teacher in this case, with that crazy story of rape, but nothing will be gained and you will not escape, believe me. You will not win. You even risk losing a great deal. Was it your idea? Was it the Mayor's? Basically, it doesn't matter anymore. You're all shits. You're talking to a specialist.

"What I want to say to you is that you can't turn the clock back. I don't know how it will all end, badly no doubt, but it will be up to you to pick up the broken pieces. I shall be far away and I'll forget you very quickly.

"You're all bastards, as I've told you, but not to the extent that you don't give a shit about anything, like me. I suspect that there's still a bit of that absurd Christian core about you that has brought in a tidy sum ever since the business at Golgotha about sin and forgiveness. That's what will finish you. You're not sufficiently detached. You don't have the spiritual means to pursue your filthy ambitions. If you want to enter the Devil's service, you have to love fire and not be afraid of being roasted in its flames. You've remained at a halfway point because you have a corrupt soul, but you don't have the balls. You're uncouth amateurs.

You'll suffer the consequences. You'll die in expiation and remorse, I'm sure of that."

The Superintendent poured himself a glass of liqueur. He made a face as he swallowed it. He glanced around the walls and suppressed a chuckle:

"Have you read all those books that surround you?"

"Some of them."

"What good did they do you?"

"They helped me understand things."

"Pray tell me, what things."

"Men. Life. The world."

"Nothing else? Pretentious! And on top of it, you come up with this miserable put-up job? Books haven't done you much good. This story of rape that doesn't stand up, except for the gathering of overexcited idiots assembled in the square, who would have swallowed it, given that it was served up on a plate? I could have called on the girl and her father before coming to see you. Three slaps would have been enough and they would probably have come up with a new version: one for the girl, who would tell me that she had lied because her father had asked her to do so, and one for her scoundrel of a father, who would admit to me that it was he who had groped her and violated her for months, which the Mayor knew about because he had once surprised him on his boat, or elsewhere, and that he had asked him to accuse the Teacher in exchange for his absolution. I would have left them both in tears, a little whore and an Australopithecus who deserved to be castrated and have both hands amputated.

"Did you want to blackmail this poor Teacher, prevent him from speaking, from telling me about what you had plotted with the three corpses that had been washed ashore, and what he discovered afterwards during his boat trips? It failed. You should have come up with something more convincing. Don't make that face, he told me everything; but, in any case, I knew more before even setting foot on your shitty island!"

He paused, inspected his cigar which had gone out, sniffed at it, and then sniffed all around him. He stared into the Doctor's eyes.

"Now you mention it, it's true that there's a stench, but I have a feeling that it's coming from you!"

XXIV

THE DOCTOR LISTENED TO THE SUPERINTENDENT, WHO was polishing off the bottle of *citron* liqueur as well as his cigar. He wondered what threads connected this fanatical creature to life. Was it indifference, love of work well done, cruelty, a loathing for his fellow man, or an unsatisfied fondness for murder, as he had confided to the Mayor, the pleasure of destroying?

He had said that he came to look for the Doctor because he saw in him someone who was less governed by his emotions than the Mayor, and to whom he would be able to explain his comments. But the Doctor felt that his visit had more to do with a strategy of intimidation. It was important for him to spread fear in small doses, just as one pours salt into an open wound so as to draw tears, in the hope that a little while later the tenderised meat will cook and cut more easily.

The Superintendent had not challenged the Teacher when he had tried to explain his discoveries to him.

"I even supplied him with information that he did not have," he said, tapping the ash of his cigar into an empty pocket that was never meant for this purpose.

"I work for people who have significant economic interests, and part of their activities concerns the area of maritime transport. My employers deal with all commodities likely to be bought and resold. They've done so for decades. Raw materials, fruit and vegetables, cars, cigarettes, consumer goods, et cetera. They are trying to be part of a global economic activity, and to adapt to the market, which as you know is frequently changing.

"The laws of different nations are excessively strict, and they do not correspond in any way to those of the market, and to its constraints. My clients therefore have to find ways of satisfying their customers by complying as best they can with these laws, which is why they like discretion. Without discretion, nothing is possible. And they are prepared to do anything to maintain this discretion. You understand me, I think?"

The Superintendent spoke like a bank employee, an accountant or a politician. Perhaps he was, in fact, all these things? To hear him speak, you could persuade yourself that he believed in what he was saying, and in spite of his totally neutral tone, you sensed nevertheless a threat underlying his every word, just as on certain pathways that meander along the foot of the Brau you suspect that a scorpion may be hiding beneath every stone.

"And then new claims arise, depending on the turmoil in the world. In recent years, unstable situations, civil wars, the unequal distribution of wealth, and famines have led to huge migratory movements from the south to the north. My employers, who are not insensitive to human distress, realised that the official international organisations were snowed under. They then tried to do their best to enable tens of thousands of men, women and children to reach what to them seemed like new promised lands.

We often downplay this aspect: the intentions of my employers and of those like them are not merely mercenary. They are also, dare I say it, perhaps first and foremost, humanitarian. I can see that this astonishes you, but I'm not asking you to believe me. I couldn't care less about your opinion and what you may think. I'm stating the facts, that's all, so that you should understand properly. People criticise the methods used by those who employ me for getting rid of competition or certain obstacles, methods which are, it is true, occasionally hasty. But all that is nothing compared to the countless deaths attributable to capitalism and ultra-liberalism.

"The world has become a business, as you know. It's no longer a field of knowledge. Science may have guided mankind for a time, but nowadays it's only money that matters. Possessing it, keeping it, acquiring it, making it circulate. My employers are certainly motivated by humanitarian intentions, but they are also businessmen. They try to reconcile aspirations that are often far removed from one another. But people never stop putting spokes in their wheels! Take borders, for example. Borders are an ill-considered nuisance when it's a matter of saving lives, don't you agree? My employers have therefore devised discreet sea routes, to enable the largest possible number of these wretched people to reach the promised land, without being prevented from doing so by administrative quibbling."

He refilled his own glass once more, and suddenly his voice changed. He spoke more slowly, and he now sounded groggy.

"Everything was going fine, until a little while ago. And then some problems arose. Problems that may appear slight, but which have nevertheless disturbed the fine harmony of what was imagined by my employers, and have eroded the trust people may have had in them, primarily that of their future clients. And that, as you can imagine, they very much resent.

"Let us suppose, to simplify matters, that certain individuals, who have none of their experience, their know-how and their dependability, tried to offer the same services as them. Not only did those who sent me suffer a shortfall – negligible, initially, though it could increase – but what's more, and above all, some incidents occurred: the three corpses that you discovered on the beach testify to this. It's regrettable. How, after such events, can you retain the vital trust of customers? Right? And how can you continue to work with the greatest discretion, a discretion on which my superiors pathologically set great store? I have come here simply to warn you. To tell you that we know. To say that enough is enough."

XXV

TO BE FRANK, THE DOCTOR UNDERSTOOD ONLY INSTINCTIVELY. He could hear the threats. He guessed, without the Superintendent ever having mentioned their name, who his employers, whose altruistic qualities he had never stopped extolling, actually were. He knew that nobody, on the island or anywhere else, wanted to get in their way and thwart their intentions.

Like everyone else, he knew their methods and their capabilities only too well. They formed a state within the state, they employed a number of people, and they got rid of a number of others who were in their way without a qualm, and in sufficiently barbarous ways for them to be impressed upon people's minds and effect a learning curve.

Their organisation was often compared to an octopus, which always upset him because the octopus is the gentlest animal there is; it's affable, it gets on well with the other creatures of the marine world, and it spends most of its life as a recluse, in some deep cavity, sheltered from everyone's gaze and causing no harm.

But what the Doctor did not understand was why the bogus policeman saw the island as the grain of sand in the commercial mechanism dreamed up by those who had sent him? How did the fact that three corpses had washed up on the shore make the islanders competitors who had to be got rid of?

"Either you're a moron, or else things are being hidden from you, while you think you know everything. And if things are being hidden from you, it's because people take you for a moron."

The Superintendent put down his glass, almost reluctantly, and picked up the threadbare leather briefcase at his feet. From it he took a bundle of papers which he placed on the Doctor's desk.

"I assume that the Mayor has circulated those that I left with him? Here are some more. You will no doubt be impressed by their quality and their precision. The famous eye of God – but God has many eyes these days, always open, which look at us constantly. You only have to knock at the right door to piece together what his eyes have seen. My employers have many connections, it's not difficult for them. Go on, take your time."

He stepped backwards, grabbed the bottle and served himself. He knocked back his glass in a gulp and smiled.

The photographs were of two types. On half of them you could see what had taken place on the actual morning of the discovery of the bodies, the various characters involved, easily identifiable, and the different things that happened: various people standing around the tarpaulin, in a circle, you might have thought that a prayer was being said around an improvised altar; then the departure of the Old Woman, of her dog, of the Teacher, of the Doctor, of America and of Swordy; the arrival of Swordy with the cart; Swordy and the Mayor lifting up the tarpaulin and loading the bodies onto the cart.

The second batch of photographs reeled off a tragic film in four acts, containing ellipses which enhanced the speed and thus increased its dizzying effect even more.

The first of these showed a boat on which dozens of black men were standing huddled together, so much so that one could not see either the bridge of the boat or its cockpit, nothing that would have enabled it to be recognised. On the second photograph, one could still see lots of men clustered together towards the stern of the boat, but the bow and part of the bridge could now be seen. The surface of the sea, which had appeared uniformly blue on the first photograph, was studded with dark dots on the second image, spread around the bow of the boat. On the third photo, the number of black dots had increased two or three times, and nothing other than two white men could be seen on the bridge – the bridge that was painted in that Tyrian pink so characteristic of the island, since all the boats are painted like that, to the extent that it is a signature, a means of recognition, and of pride too – two white men who were holding in their hands something that could have been a gun, a truncheon or part of a harpoon. On the last photograph, the boat had made a manoeuvre and tacked about, and all one could see was its stern, the rest of it being out of the frame. In the blue water, the black dots were still numerous, and some of them showed arms raised towards the boat that was sailing away. You could see them, these raised arms. Arms raised towards the man who was now gazing at the image, the man who had recognised the boat and had guessed that the two men were fishermen from the island.

The Superintendent filled his glass again and pushed it towards the Doctor.

"I think you have more need of it than I do. You're very pale.

What did you say to me not ten minutes ago, about all your books? That they have taught you about the world, about life and mankind? Well, you haven't read the right ones and, in spite of your age, a large part of your education still remains to be acquired."

The Doctor knocked back his drink. The alcohol filled his throat with a fierce fire. He pushed the photographs away as if discarding them would be enough to make what they depicted disappear. His head was spinning. The Superintendent put them away in his briefcase.

"Strange sort of fishermen, you must admit, who throw away the product of their catch without any compunction. And why did they do all this? Because of a patrol boat which they had probably taken for a coastguard vessel and which in actual fact was merely involved in peddling cigarettes – I am in a position to know this – and which had followed them for a short while just to give them a fright."

The Superintendent drew on his cigar and gazed at the embers, and the smoke which he slowly exhaled.

"What a waste! So many dead because of an error, for a bit of contraband tobacco!"

He got to his feet.

"I must leave you. I must pack my bag. I've fulfilled my mission. I'm setting off tomorrow. There's nothing left for me to do on your rock. I feel as though I've been here for a thousand years. Nothing happens here. Time just stands still. You'll have to sort things out yourselves from now on. You've got a lot to do. Up to you to settle your own scores. I don't think you'll have any difficulty in finding out who those two idiots were. It no longer concerns me. But don't oblige me to come back, me or someone like me. There's a limit to our patience. No-one paid any attention to you until recently. Make sure that it becomes like that again."

The Superintendent was one of those people whom nobody notices and who go through life without making much of an impact. The unlikelihood of his existence was further reinforced shortly after his departure.

He was seen boarding the ferry on Tuesday morning. Several witnesses, starting with the Café Owner, swore they had seen him getting on board. The Captain did not say otherwise, even if he was less positive, detained as he was at that moment by a leaking engine.

What is undisputed, on the other hand, is that the Superintendent did not disembark on the mainland. He had vanished during the crossing, like the smoke from his cigar. Whether he disappeared or threw himself overboard, or whether his employers, so concerned with discretion, as he had repeated time and again, had done away with him, is of no importance. For the inhabitants of the island, his life had only lasted a few days. Before this time, he had not existed. Afterwards, he no longer existed.

The brevity of the Superintendent's life resembled the lives of the three washed-up bodies. For them, ironically, it was the moment of their deaths that caused them to exist for the islanders, so much so that they live on still and always will, unbearable and accusatory, with every passing hour.

XXVI

THE MAYOR WAS STANDING IN FRONT OF THE DOCTOR. Both of them were silent. Both of them were on their feet. The Doctor was no longer smiling. The Mayor had not often seen him like this. Without his smile. Without the ridiculous dye with which he daubed his moustache. Without his elegant crumpled linen suit. It was Tuesday morning. It was not yet seven o'clock. The Doctor was wearing casual trousers and an old sweater, over green pyjamas that protruded at the ankles and wrists. The Mayor had put on a grey dressing gown. Grey like his hair. Grey like his skin. Grey like his eyes.

Two statues standing side by side, with a huge gap separating them, apparently unaware of the small space between them in the attractive room inside the Mayor's house.

"And those two men on the bridge, did you recognise them?"

"No."

"Are you sure?"

"Certain."

"That shit must have other photographs. Photographs in which they could be recognised."

"Of course."

"Then why weren't they shown to us?"

"So that the suspicion should be complete. So that no-one should be spared. Those two men, they could be anybody. It could be you. Your neighbour. Anyone here. Why not me? That's what he wanted. To ruin all our days for us. Ruin our lives. So that we all look at one another wondering who did that."

"The bastard!"

"Make sure it's the right bastard."

"What are we going to do?"

The Doctor thought before he answered. And his response was the one you find in books, too well phrased, too striking and true for him to have been able to dream it up on this bedraggled morning. He had probably spent the whole night polishing it up, as sleep evaded him.

"We shall all have to live with the suspicion, and do so until the hour of our death."

The Mayor weighed up his remark. He looked down at the floor. He replied in a quiet voice:

"But you, you know me. You know very well I'm incapable of such a monstrous thing. Throwing wretched people into the sea!"

"I know you," replied the Doctor, by which he meant everything as well as its opposite, but the Mayor was happy to twist the Doctor's words in the way that suited him. He had hoped for absolution. The Doctor continued:

"But how would you describe what you did to the Teacher?"

During the night, the Brau had once again reminded people of its existence. It had rumbled, a very long rumbling, not very distinct and almost pleasant, in fact, just as the caress of a massage machine can be when it soothes the soles of one's feet, or one's painful vertebrae.

During this astonishing morning, while the Mayor and the Doctor stood there in silence, the Brau began to rumble again, but this time impatiently. It was a sort of short bark that caused the walls and the furniture to move, the doors to creak and three plates to fall off the Mayor's dresser. They shattered on the ground between the feet of the two men, who were both wearing the same slippers. They gazed at the scattered pieces of china, the sharp corners and white rim which had been suddenly caught in the light and looked phosphorescent. Then they gazed at one another. Each wondered whether something else had not just been shattered irretrievably between them.

They spoke about the Teacher once more and of the fate that had been agreed for him. They had lit a flame that would not easily be put out. Dozens of men and women had continued to sleep in the town square, impromptu guardians of a prisoner who they believed was accountable to them and on whom they demanded to pass judgement, and on whom, through the window of the cellar where he was being held, they had not stopped heaping insults.

"Could you take another look at your report on the girl?"

"All I did was write the truth. She hasn't been a virgin for a long while."

"I know that as well as you do. But I also know that the Teacher has got nothing to do with it."

"What did you promise the girl?"

"Nothing. She loathes the Teacher. He stands for everything she lacks at home, gentleness, affection, goodness. She must have dreamed of being in his daughters' shoes, but she's Furry's daughter. Life is a lottery, as we all know. It's enough to make people want to do harm. Some begin early. Childhood is not always a bed of roses."

"It's up to you to persuade her to tell the truth now. You alone created this situation."

"I did it for all of us."

"No-one asked you to do so, but if that's what you like to think . . . In any case, there will always be people here who will continue to believe the Teacher is guilty, whatever you do, whatever you say. He has to leave. Quickly. The island is no longer the place for him. That's what you really wanted, isn't it?"

"The island was never the place for him. It's hardly the place for us any longer."

The Mayor bent down and began picking up the broken bits of plate.

"Are you planning to stick them together?"

"Why say such stupid things?"

They were obliged to call on the Teacher in order to release him. The Doctor agreed to accompany the Mayor. They gave each other a brief moment to wash and change, and also to enable the Mayor to call at Furry's home and talk to the girl. They met afterwards outside the church, opposite the town hall, in the already intense heat of the day that was barely a few hours old. The sky no longer existed, lost as it was in a flat leadenness consisting of smooth, high clouds which the sun had heated without really showing itself. They could hear the ferry's siren as the ship left port, taking the Superintendent away for ever.

When those who had camped out on the square caught sight of the Mayor and the Doctor, they approached them. The night and their hatred had contorted their faces, making them look like old scraps of crumpled paper. The men's cheeks were dotted with black hairs. The women's had taken on the colour of dish-water in the midst of which two red eyes and parched lips revealed abstract features. They all smelled and were all tainted with the same fever that made them long for death; a fever that had probably plagued those who watched at scaffolds once upon a time, who, as the heads fell off and the blood gushed, were suddenly provided with a brutal direction to their lives, a lungful of power and pleasure.

The Mayor's words did very little to calm them. In a way, they deprived them of the person who, within a few hours, had become the reason for their existence. They had been robbed. They had been pick-pocketed. What did it matter to them to know that the girl's remarks had been misunderstood, that the Doctor was no longer sure of anything, that the Superintendent himself had exonerated the accused?

Certain words create walls that other words never manage to break down. The Mayor told them to go back to their homes. But at home there was nothing but a daily newspaper crammed with tedium and rehashed items, monotonous and already familiar, which had already done the rounds and made them feel ill. Whereas there, on the town square, they suddenly felt different. It's very tough to come back down from one's dreams.

The Mayor took the precaution of locking the door of the town hall as soon as they were inside. He slowly climbed the main stairs to his office, where he made some coffee. The Doctor watched him. Neither of them said a word. Their minds were filled with all the images that the Superintendent had planted in them. Then, still without a word being exchanged, they went down to the cellar. The Mayor held a cup of coffee in one hand

and a bunch of keys in the other. The Doctor was fingering his first cigar, which he had not yet lit. He had not yet managed to display his well-known smile on his plump, round face. Just as he had given up dyeing his moustache. Paradoxically, this made him look younger and more frail.

The Mayor knocked at the door of the cellar, not so much to obtain permission to enter as to warn the Teacher of their arrival, perhaps so that he would have time to rearrange his clothing. He put in the key and fiddled with the lock. He pushed open the door ready to greet him, but the words remained stuck in his throat: at the foot of the makeshift bed, his eyes closed and his face slightly blue, lay the Teacher.

No-one could have been more dead than he.

XXVII

WHAT IS SHAME, AND HOW MANY PEOPLE ARE AFFECTED by it? Is it shame that connects men to humanity? Or does it merely underline the fact that they are irreversibly removed from it?

They had killed the Teacher. It has to be said. They did not kill him with their own hands, of course, but they had constructed his death, in the way that one builds a wall, stone by stone. Each one of them had brought his own stone, or prepared the mortar, pushed the wheelbarrow, carried a bucket of water, held the trowel, poured a little sand into cement that was too watery.

His death was a shared deed.

His wife was clearly not mistaken when, on the following night, a night of pain and incredulity, she knocked with both fists on every door, not so much in order that they should be opened to her, as to indicate that, behind every door that remained closed, there was a guilty person inside. She spat on every door, not omitting a single one of them, as she yelled wolf-like cries in every small street of the town, pouring out her fury in a language that did not consist of words but of death rattles. Her two little daughters followed in silence, their faces pale and calm, like a tragic escort, holding each other's hand.

Only one door opened to her knocking. That of the Old Woman. The Old Woman, who stood before the Teacher's wife, who said nothing to her, who looked her in the eye, who said nothing when the woman spat in her face, who still said nothing when the woman slapped her, five times, slaps that were like punches, which caused the Old Woman to stagger but not to fall down. And the Old Woman continued to stand there, with spittle on her forehead and cheeks, the reddish marks of the blows on her temples and cheekbones, and an eyelid that swelled up and turned violet, while the woman and her two little girls resumed their implacable procession and the night gulped them down like bitter milk.

Had the Old Woman opened her door in atonement? So that, in this way, she alone could represent the island? So as to take the place of each and every one of them. She had offered herself up to the woman's fury and her blows, for the sake of everyone. In their place. In their name. But the Old Woman may not have been bothered about anything other than herself; her gesture had no hint of nobility about it, and if she had opened the door, it was only to show that she herself was very much alive and alright, and was not blaming herself for anything, to let people know that she had both her feet on the ground and that the fuss about the Teacher's wife did not affect her, and would not prevent her from living.

When the Doctor hurried over to the corpse, he could not help noticing how cold and stiff it was. The Teacher had been dead for many hours. His blond, curly hair contrasted sharply with the colour of his skin, which was not pale, but had a slightly bluish tinge with blotches here and there, which made the Doctor realise that the wretched man had died from asphyxiation.

The thing responsible for this stood immediately beside the body, huge and parallelepipedal, haughty in its metal corset, its jaws open wide above its throat filled with flying sparks, diffusing its carbon monoxide breath, invisible and odourless, around the dim space of the enclosed cellar.

The Mayor, who had also realised what had happened, rushed over to the basement window, which had been completely obstructed by a thick blanket and plastic sacks. The Teacher had probably done this in order to try to muffle the insults that the crowd outside was yelling at him, as though directly into his ear. He was far from being an idiot. He was aware of the boiler being there and of the dangers of gas, but it is difficult to believe that he should consciously have acted in this way and chosen to die like this. He was weak. He was exhausted. His thoughts were no longer clear, and whose would have been in his position? He did not want to die. He had not assessed the consequences of what he was doing.

The Doctor pushed the door wide open. The air, which had been poisoned by the fumes from the boiler, immediately cleared. The Mayor gazed at the corpse, incredulous and panic-stricken. He was probably telling himself that the Teacher was proving to be even more of a nuisance dead than he had been alive. That was his triumph, basically, because the dead, whatever anybody says, are always right.

The Secretary, who had just arrived, was sent to find the Priest. She was made up and fragrant as though she was going to a ball, but nothing was said to her other than that the Priest was needed. He came immediately. Curiously, not a single bee accompanied him. He did not seem surprised, but he looked profoundly saddened. He stood in silence before the corpse, which had been put back on the bed. He did not say any prayers, make the sign of the cross, or bless the Teacher's body. After a long and heavy pause, he turned to the Doctor and the Mayor:

"Can you smell him now?"

"Who?" asked the Mayor.

"Him," said the Priest, pointing to the dead man. "Your new lodger. He is here," he continued, tapping his skull with his forefinger. "In each of your heads. He has just moved in. He's not going to leave. From now on, he will remain with you until the end of your lives. Day and night. He won't be at all noisy, but you will never be able to evict him. You'll have to get used to it. Good luck."

And having wiped his thick spectacles with his cassock, he left them both there, to ruminate on these remarks from an estate-agent philosopher, before going to inform those who did not yet know that, during the night, they had become a widow and orphans.

XXVIII

THERE IS A RUSSIAN NOVEL THAT DESCRIBES A CITY deserted by all its inhabitants. We are not told the reason why they have fled. The author remains enigmatic: war, disease, nuclear incident. We know nothing. We never will. The time period is not specified either. The city is undamaged, but empty. The doors of the houses are not closed. Anyone can go inside.

The author shows them around the houses, in a series of long descriptions that can be boring. Life has receded from the city like a wave drawn away by the backwash. In many of the houses the table has been set, in the kitchen or the drawing room. Bread has been laid out. Water in the jugs. The dishes are in saucepans, placed over extinguished burners.

The food has not rotted, and it is as though their departure only took place a minute earlier. Here and there, a chair has been knocked over, or a cupboard left open, both of which are evidence of the hurried exodus of the inhabitants.

Such is the first part of the novel, which takes readers into a great many streets, and leads them inside a great many houses. A strange atmosphere then takes hold, like that of a dream, a curious dream where we are not sure whether it is pleasant or disturbing.

The reader finds himself almost drifting off, but continues his visit over the course of a hundred pages or so; and when suddenly, on entering the corridor of a building at the invitation of the author, he discovers a man busily trying to open a letter box, he experiences a profound shock. Everything until now had been the setting and the surroundings, inert things, and here, all of a sudden, was a man. A man busily engaged in a simple task, collecting his post.

But the man is struggling to open the door of the letter box. He does not have the key. We tell ourselves that he may be trying the wrong letter box, but he perseveres, even though he still has not managed to open it. In the end he gives up, goes upstairs, enters the first apartment and walks around it. Then he enters the second, and then the next one.

All of a sudden we wonder who he is and what he can be doing here. He is not a thief. He is not stealing anything, even though he frequently touches things, such as the fabrics, and picks up picture frames and stares at the photographs. His face remains expressionless.

As he leaves the building and as he enters another house, he comes upon another man. Or rather, the reader discovers this second man, because the first one does not appear to see him, just as the second one doesn't see the first. They jostle one another, but take no notice of the other person.

And the novel continues, some women appear, some children, old people and other men. The town fills up with this new throng of people, silent and speechless, who have the distinctive feature of consisting of individuals who are totally indifferent to one another and are invisible to others. Only the reader can see them.

Then he understands. Or rather, the author lets him understand. He makes him realise that they are all dead. That none of them see one another. That the town has become the city of the dead. We don't know whether there are still any people who are alive, somewhere. But however that may be, this particular town is no longer for them. It belongs solely to the dead. They have chosen to come here, if not to live here then at least to frequent it. It thus becomes a dreadful town. A town that is impossible to live in. On closing the book, the reader feels frightened.

On the night following the death of the Teacher, the little town was deserted. Its inhabitants driven away. Buried. Vanished. Disbanded within the thick walls of their houses. The doors on which the Widow had pounded with her fists, her fists and her yells, all shut.

And today, the island has become the town in the Russian novel. The soil is dead, due to the incandescent vomiting of the Brau, the waters are stagnant and contain nothing but the wreckage of boats. The hours, which bring neither joy nor hope, are lifeless. Only the dead now make themselves at home, in the streets, in the houses, in the squares, around the harbour. The Teacher, the three young black men who were drowned, their fellows in their thousands, countless numbers, swallowed up by the waves or pushed overboard. The town is too small for all of them. The island is too small. They walk along the streets, dripping wet and silent, without hatred or anger. They are unaware of the others, but the others see them. They remind them who they are and who they would not have wished to be.

The ferry carried away the Teacher's coffin, and his wife and his little daughters. The ferry did not sound its siren. On either side of the coffin, the Teacher's wife and his twin girls were staring at the harbour, the town, the volcano, the island. They were staring at all of this with their eyes of stone. The houses were still closed up. The residents absent. Invisible. Only the Priest had accompanied them to the port. And he had remained there, watching the ferry disappear, the silent ferry with the Widow and the little girls, and the coffin, at the stern, and inside the coffin the body of a man who, for his part, had tried his best to merit the name of man.

It took a few days for people to start acting normally again. To try to pick up the ordinary course of events once more. Everyone behaved as they knew how. Unimportant comments were exchanged. No-one ever spoke again about the Teacher, even though people thought about him constantly, even though what the Priest had said to the Mayor and the Doctor proved to be appallingly accurate.

Similarly, between the Mayor and the Doctor the matter of the boat and its tragic human cargo that the satellite had photographed was never mentioned again. Without consulting one another, they had decided not to say anything and not to know anything more about it. Not to attempt to recognise the boat on the photographs, or the two men. Only the Priest was informed, but this had been in the secrecy of the confessional, and he, not believing in very much any longer, possibly not even in God, respected his vow of silence and did not repeat to anyone what the Mayor had confided in him in this way.

For it was he, the Mayor, who, beneath his air of ruling with a rod of iron, regularly felt the need to flush out his soul to the Priest, not so much to obtain from him some sort of forgiveness, but because the simple mind of a man can never retain all the evil that is deposited in it and which it exudes, and because this regular bloodletting soothed him for a while, and enabled him to put up with himself and put up with the world.

For one had to go on living. Living while knowing all the while that within this community there also lived slave-drivers, men who traded in human bodies, dealers in dreams, robbers of hope, murderers. People who, because they thought themselves hounded, had not hesitated to toss dozens of their fellow men into the waters of the Saliva of the Dog, where they all drowned. These men were here, close at hand, these men who murdered other men.

XXIX

TEN DAYS AFTER THE FERRY HAD CARRIED AWAY THE remains of the Teacher, his Widow and his twin girls, Biceps set off very slowly towards the bench at the far end of the jetty. The S'tunella bench.

Biceps was the senior fisherman. He lied a little when he said he was more than a hundred years old, but he can't have been far off that age. People called him Biceps because in his youth he had apparently possessed remarkable muscles, which he exhibited whenever anyone asked. No-one was around to remember this, and these days Biceps was little more than a slim collection of frail bones, a bit of dry skin and a great many wrinkles. A walking stick made from one of his vine stocks served as his actual leg. He could hardly see anymore, and he moved as slowly as a snail, but his mind still functioned fairly well.

He sat on the bench and waited. A few moments later, he was joined by Pearl, Siesta and Dry Arse, three other elderly fishermen whose surnames there is little point in revealing, and who walked slightly better than he did, all three of them having barely reached the age of ninety. The conference could begin.

It lasted just over an hour. An hour during which the four elderly men sat looking at the sea as they attempted to read it, to assess it, to discover whether the great shoals of tuna that come up from the south were to be found at its greatest depth, within reach of the island, within reach of the boats and the nets. The same guesswork occurred every year.

At last they could be seen getting to their feet and returning to the port, Biceps at their head, sliding rather than walking over the paving stones, rather like those robots that are given to children at Christmas and which operate on batteries for a while, then wear out. The three others didn't dare overtake him, out of respect. Almost ten minutes later, they finally reached the port where the fishermen were waiting for them in silence, bare-headed, their caps in their hands.

Biceps gathered his breath, and then spoke the ritual form of words, in a strong voice that one would not have expected from such a worn-out body:

"The moment for the S'tunella has arrived. To your boats, fishermen, and you, mothers, wives and children, pray for them!"

Normally, cries of delight and music accompany the bidding. People are happy. Bottles are opened. Some music is played. There are toasts.

Nothing of the sort took place this year. The bidding was greeted with silence, so that Biceps thought that no-one had heard it. He therefore repeated it. But there was silence once more. The fishermen put their caps back on and dispersed. They went over to their boats to make sure all their equipment was safe, then they set off home to have a final meal surrounded by their families. Each of them went to bed early. The following day, they would leave before dawn.

Many people had heard tell of the S'tunella without necessarily remembering the name. Many had probably also seen photographs, among them the best known, in which you can see fishing boats arranged in a circle, and in the midst of this circle thousands of furious tuna, which are harpooned and gaffed before being hoisted on board, while the sea takes on the colour of their blood and suddenly turns a thick red that stains the naked thighs, the torsos and the faces of the fishermen.

The S'tunella has more to do with hunting than fishing. Its origins are lost in the mists of time and of legend. It is the fledgling concept of land-bound people accustomed to hunting game, and which unforeseen events, wars or famines have driven towards the sea, upon which and in which they have attempted to perpetuate the wiles of hunting.

In this very distinctive form of catching fish, which exists nowhere else in the world, the boats are set out in a pattern similar to that which beaters adopt when they participate in big-game hunts, and which may well have been the custom when they once hunted foxes, aurochs and bison. On each of the boats, the men yell down a sort of wooden tube, the *kaffin*, the far end of which is plunged into the waves, and they beat upon the hulls of their boats with the shafts of their harpoons. The aim is to frighten the shoals of tuna, through the echoing sounds made by this din, and to drive them towards an area that would have been decided on beforehand, and upon which all the boats converge, letting their large, well-filled nets drift behind them.

This can take several days. This is when they say they beat the sea. The most experienced fishermen, what is more, can sense the reactions of this sea that has endured such a din. They say that it bristles, that it lies back and takes it, that it shudders, that it hides, that it rages, that it uses cunning or that it squeezes, according to whatever these men expect of the sea at the time, and above all what they imagine to be the movements of this fish that looks like a large cannonball, and which is known as the red tuna. The tuna, this emblem, this monarch. The greatest of fish, the one that comes to mind when one tries to draw a fish. In a perfect movement, like a child's drawing, pure, undeviating, faultless, an obvious outline that denotes genius.

The tuna's skin shows no scales. It's a fuselage. When you cut into it, you would think it was a tree. Its eye is human and it judges you. Its compact flesh is reminiscent of the muscles of a warrior. Its wounds are worthy ones. Its death is a long time in coming. When you observe these fish slipping between the currents, in their hundreds, in the translucent depths, the sun does its best to delve into the belly of the sea as far as possible, and it shines on their backs with a pewter-like grey. Unlike the shoals of garfish, scabbardfish or barracuda which frolic with the light as though it was a musical instrument – a sort of aquatic organ whose distant melody one sometimes perceives – the tuna absorbs the rays of the sun and never reflects them. It cleaves the depths, as the ploughshare does the earth. It striates the sea in the silence of its perfect outline, launched by invisible cannons, far removed from everything.

The S'tunella represents simultaneously the veneration that men feel for the tuna and its awe-inspiring death. In the arena formed by the boats when, after several days and several nights, they meet again having driven the enormous shoals before them, the final act is played out.

The large trapped fish collide with one another and hurl themselves up out of the waves, forcing their massive weight skywards, giving them the illusion that they can fly. The men on the boats fire harpoons which thrust into their compact flesh, or sometimes glide over their hard, shiny bodies, without wounding them. You would think you were witnessing a primitive scene such as those painted by the first men on the walls of caves.

What reinforces still more the parallel with an archaic activity is the custom that requires the fishermen, just as the final circle is formed, to be dressed simply in baggy white cotton shorts, the *runello*, which is more like a loincloth, and is made of one long strip of material that is wound several times around the waist and tucked in between the legs. As the tuna are harpooned and hoisted onto the boats, and as their blood spurts out, the bodies of the fishermen and the encircling sea turn red until all the white and all the blue vanishes.

Accompanying this incredible ferment of the sea created by the large fish (which curiously do not seem to realise that their salvation could be procured by diving down to the deep) – a ferment that precedes the killing and which one might think was induced by a gigantic fire created in the very depths of the sea – is the violent drunkenness caused by the blood and by death.

The fishermen kill, in a frenzy that lasts for several hours, consumed by their actions which they repeat mechanically, intoxicated by the cries they yell out to give themselves courage, and by the din caused by the beating of fins that invades their minds and shatters all thoughts, all conscience and all feeling.

And the creatures die, one after another, large, heavy bodies on which only the tails still move and whose undamaged eyes confront the eyes of the fisherman whom they can no longer see, corpses weighing a hundredweight, hoisted up with much liberating puffing and panting, and piled up on board the boats like logs, still warm from the sap of thousands of trees from a destroyed forest.

When nothing moves any longer, apart from the hulls of the ships, when the indifferent swell returns to its gentle lapping and everything is still again, a tremendous noise surges up, emanating from the exhausted fishermen, plastered with blood and sweat. Then the fish are counted and the boat on which lie the most fish becomes the flagship which will lead the flotilla back to the island, and will be the first to enter the port, to the applause of all those who remained ashore.

But beforehand, and to conclude the ceremony, the captain of this boat is proclaimed "Re dul S'tunella". He is not entitled to any crown, but he is given a baptism, which consists of plunging into the battlefield, into the bloody sea, of diving into the filthy red water, and swimming in it for a long time and emerging once more to much cheering, transformed into a barbaric creature, with blood-clotted hair, whose face can only be told apart from the rest of the body by his two staring and exhausted opaline eyes and by the whiteness of his teeth.

Tradition requires that the Re dul S'tunella should stand at the prow of his boat, and return to port in that position, without washing himself, stained with the noble blood of his victory, and that the other fishermen should also retain the marks of combat on their thighs and their arms that are the proof of their bravery.

The minds of those who have once seen the fishermen returning in this way, are engraved with images that seem to have emanated from the epics of antiquity. They thus give man the sweet and unique sense of primitive strength, of the power of life, of the gravity of death, and of the minute place that he occupies in the heart of the great theatre of the world, which occasionally deigns to open its curtain to him.

But in this sad year, there was no Re dul S'tunella.

There was no king because there was no victory.

There was not even a battle.

XXX

THE BOATS RETURNED TO PORT TEN DAYS AFTER THEY HAD left, their holds as empty as when they had set out. The sailors' bodies were not stained with any blood, but the expressions on their faces indicated both astonishment and gravity. The great nutritive fish had constantly avoided them. During the voyage they had not once heard their murmur, or spotted their muted glow.

They disembarked from their vessels without saying a word. They forced a path through the incredulous crowd on whom a great silence had descended. They returned, ashamed, to hide away in their homes. The Brau rumbled slightly, as if to show its opprobrium.

In the memory of men, they had never experienced such a thing.

People immediately began gossiping about a curse. When people don't understand certain facts, it is easy to resort to magic and the supernatural. It was whispered that the Teacher's little girls bore the expressions of witches, that they had laid a curse on the island, that the cries of the Widow on the night following the death of her husband had placed spells of vengeance and also of evil on every house. It was said that on leaving the island on the ferry, with the body of the dead man in the white poplar coffin, the Widow and the children had lured to themselves all the fish in the sea, had put a charm on them, and had led them in their ethereal nets towards other islands, other fishermen, other vessels.

They talked nonsense.

But the truth was that the boats had indeed returned without a catch. And however much the Mayor explained the disastrous campaign, mistreated his men, scolded them and treated them as though they were incompetent, however much he pored over nautical charts, spoke to Biceps and the other elderly men for hours, consulted ancient registers and gathered all the fishermen together, nothing came of any of this. Mankind is either extremely naïve or very conceited to imagine that any mystery can be understood, and that any problem can be resolved.

The Doctor no longer went anywhere without a handkerchief over his nose. The stench had increased still more. It was no longer merely a smell, it was becoming a taste. He felt as though he were still breathing it and chewing it. The others could not detect anything of this smell of decaying carcass and rotting meat. The Old Woman shrugged whenever she passed him, and the Mayor placed his index finger on the side of his head whenever the Doctor tried to talk to him about it. He seldom went out.

In his sleep, the three young men who had drowned came to visit him, they lay down beside him, or they remained standing at the back of the room. The water dripped from the bottom of their trouser legs and formed a puddle on the wooden floor. The pool grew larger. The water rose along the sides of the walls. It swept through the room up to the ceiling. He died in it without dying. He was floating. He was carried off by the young black men, into deep currents. He was joined by the Teacher, whose blond hair looked like sponges. He smiled at him a little sadly, as he had done the day after the secret meeting at the town hall that had followed the discovery of the corpses. He had encountered him in the street. It was morning. The Teacher had just returned from running. He stopped, somewhat out of breath, and said:

"You didn't help me much yesterday evening."

The Doctor had shrugged.

"Yet you're intelligent. I was depending on you. And I'm sure that you're a good man."

"I'm a cowardly man above all," he had said.

"A cowardly man?" the Teacher had responded, dreamily.

"It's almost a pleonasm, isn't it?" the Doctor had concluded.

In his darkness, the journey continued towards the high seas. He drifted among other drowned people and among thousands of tuna that bore quizzical expressions. They all ended up in large black nets, in the midst of a circle of boats. They were harpooned. He felt the tip of the arrow entering his side, going right through him, glancing off a vertebrae, smashing a bone and puncturing viscera. Yet he was not in pain. And then he was hoisted up.

Whereupon he woke up, contemplating the last words written by Arthur Rimbaud, the nineteenth-century French poet, a volume of whose work never left his bedside. While his leg was being amputated and he lay dying in a hospital room not far from the port of Marseilles, Rimbaud had written a brief letter to the captain of the ship which he still hoped to embark, to return to Abyssinia. It ended with this sentence:

"Let me know at what time I shall be carried on board."

Everyone asks themselves this question sooner or later, but everyone behaves nevertheless as though they were carrying on.

The Doctor and the Mayor were putting the finishing touches to the Thermal file, but their hearts were no longer in it. Without admitting it, they knew that the project would never see the light of day. Without giving in to the belief that a curse would befall the island, they both had a premonition that it and its shores would be cluttered by too many corpses. The presence of these dead people put a strain on the living, and took from them not so much the will to live, as their love and hope in life. All this was like a stain on a piece of clothing, on clothing that one had enjoyed wearing.

They spent long periods of time together, but something had been damaged, both between them and within their world. The Brau made its voice heard increasingly frequently. There were scarcely any days when you did not feel its irritated shudder beneath your feet and inside the houses and hear its elderly predator's roar.

The sky sulked above them. The sun no longer appeared. The heat was no less suffocating. It wrung them out like washing. It seemed to them as though they were entering an endless season of boiling temperatures and darkness. It was not yet the isle of the dead, exactly, but it was already the isle of the dying.

That autumn, the grapes that had been laid out to dry turned into ash-coloured berries. When they were squeezed, a dark juice was emitted that had a taste of burnt wood. The wine made from them was second-rate.

Before Christmas, one family left the island: the father, the skipper of the small company that the unproductive S'tunella had ruined, the mother and the children. They were the first. There would be many others.

America, who had lost all his vines, which had been burned before being cut, went and took a job on the mainland. It is said that he now looks after the paths in a former zoo. Perhaps the one that the Superintendent visited when he was a child.

They discovered Swordy hanging one morning in the cold room where he and the Mayor had laid out the bodies of the drowned. He looked like a large stalactite, such as one sees beneath the roofs of chalets in illustrated books of Norse fables, but as one drew closer to the stalactite, one noticed his bulging expression beneath the thick layer of ice, his mouth slightly ajar and his tongue which was sticking out.

He had written a brief note to explain his departure and it was attached to his jacket with a fishhook. But when they let the ice melt around his body, the water diluted the ink, and all that remained of his message were the first words, "I know who", and that was all. He knew. He knew who. So what. It had not saved him.

The Old Woman, without asking anybody anything, started her classes again. Her knife-like silhouette and her blank expression could be seen through the school windows. Boys and girls listened to her, fearful and embarrassed. She taught them about a lost world of which they did not understand a thing. Many of them probably thought of the Teacher, in a mood of regret, their youthful memories recalling his smile and his gentle voice, and all the current knowledge that he knew how to impart to them. Mila probably thought about him too. The Doctor came across her occasionally in the streets, her father, with his false hair askew, always drunk, holding her by the hand not in the way one should hold one's young daughter, but in the way you would lead a woman or a victim to your home. The Doctor looked away.

Then very soon, with the departure of most of the families, there were no more children. So there was no more school. The Old Woman buried herself away in her home, with her dog, which had become so old that it could only manage to drag itself about outside a little with its front feet, in the courtyard, and both of them waited there. They weren't sure what for.

There were no more boats at the quay. The waters of the archipelago were well and truly dead. The fish had fled from them as though they had become unhealthy. The fishermen must have gone into self-imposed exile, to follow shoals elsewhere, far away. Far from the island. Only the eldest among them, those whose lives were already over, stayed behind.

All the crops disappeared beneath the streams of slow and dough-like lava that the Brau vomited out over two days the following spring, driving it as far as the doors of the first houses, reshaping the landscape, covering it with a thick and furrowed coat that caused the entire geography of the past to disappear.

The few vines and orchards on Ross Hill that had escaped the streams of magma dried up during the weeks that followed and never turned green again. The Brau drank their sap, charred their roots and poisoned them. All that remained of what had been the splendour and richness of the island for centuries were the rows of naked vine stocks on the bare hillock, grey stumps eroded by the termites, and leafless bushes on which even the sparrows did not deign to perch. The little town was sealed off by high, dark, congealed folds, resembling another sea, harsh and dead, sterile for eternity.

The Priest died not long after his bees. He watched his swarms perish for lack of flowers from which to gather nectar and pollen. He filled the pockets of his cassock with all the dried-up bodies with their delicate wings that he found by the hives every morning. He returned to his presbytery in tears. He lay the bodies on his kitchen table. They formed a pale-brown mound. He spent his last days beside this chitinous pyramid, watching over the dead bees, praying for the salvation of their souls, for he had begun to believe in God once more, ever since the events that had occurred, interpreting them as the sign of a curse sent from On High to strike down all the inhabitants of the island, him first of all, who had enjoyed himself over so many years in the constant doubt of his Garden of Olives.

After three days had passed, he crammed all the dead bees into his frying pan in large shovelfuls, and burned them. When this was done, he lay down on his bed, fully dressed. He died during the night, his hands clasping his rosary and his missal which he had placed on his stomach, with his thick-lensed glasses over his closed eyes.

No doubt there is a place in the Paradise in which he still believed a little, assigned to women's high jump contests, a curve in the stadium where he will be standing on the terraces, accompanied by a few bees, admiring for all eternity the shapely legs and slim waists of the young women despatched too early, and who attempt, in graceful and sensuous arched movements, to topple over death in order to re-join life.

*

The church was closed; it had become a strange sort of ark, with its skeleton of a boat, but one in which no animal's cry was ever heard, and where Noah continually failed to appear.

Yet the Flood had well and truly taken place.

XXXI

THERE WE ARE. WE'RE ALMOST DONE. I HAVE APPROACHED the edge of the abyss to tell the story. It's about to conclude. Creeping backwards, I shall fade away.

I shall return to the shadows.

I shall dissolve myself there.

I shall have left you the words. I will take away the silences.

I shall disappear.

I had promised you to be no more than the voice.

Nothing else.

All the rest is human and concerns you.

It is not my problem.

Time has passed on the island but it has sorted out nothing. That is not its function. Ovid wrote that time destroys things, but he was wrong. Only men destroy things, and they destroy men, and destroy the world of men. Time watches them do and undo. It flows indifferently, just as the lava flowed from the crater of the Brau one March evening, cloaking the island in darkness and driving the last living people from it.

Just as, in former times, a black armband was placed on a

person in mourning, the earth now wears the colour of the dead, and that of funerals. This will endure for thousands of years. One way or another, there has to be a punishment.

The Doctor spent several months in bed, with a powerful fever. Yet he showed no sign of pathology. He was slightly delirious. His mind was confused. He shivered even when it was very hot outside. He treated himself with herbal teas of thyme and small glasses of warm marc to which he added sugar. He had hypnotic dreams, either filled with visions, or very dark like the empty spaces of the universe.

He got better. Everything returned to normal again. His first visit was to the Mayor. One morning.

The Doctor found the Mayor changed. He had suddenly grown older. His complexion had become yellow. His grey hair had turned white. You would have thought that it had snowed on him. He had never been very stout but he now floated in his trousers and his shirts. He had sold his boats and closed his warehouses. He was still Mayor, but Mayor of what?

He poured coffee into the cups. The Doctor could hear the Mayor's wife preparing the meal in the room next door. They wanted him to stay for breakfast as usual, but as usual he would refuse and would transport his large body home to feed himself on a little bread, olives and solitude.

"Do you know the dream I woke myself up with today?" the Doctor said in order to fill the silence.

"How do you expect me to know? I'm not inside your head."

"Fortunately for you. You're lucky."

"Would you prefer to be inside mine?"

The Mayor had spoken with an air of sad defiance. The Doctor replied with a smile, with sadness too.

"It was a dream that was just like a nightmare, but which was not frightening, even though it was filled with horror. You and I had been summoned, I don't know by whom, to go to the beach, as on that fateful morning long ago. And we arrived there together, you had called by to collect me, or the other way round, I'm not sure and it matters little. We had tried to run or to walk as quickly as possible. We were out of breath, I smoke too much, I'm too fat, my feet hurt me, and you're just skin and bones, with no strength. We made a strange couple of runners.

"The weather was grey. The sky very low. The Brau invisible in its cloak of clouds, and the sea appeared irritated, with small, nervous waves that smacked into one another and struck the shingle. There were some large stranded shapes, lifeless and tossing about, perhaps four, five or six of them, we could not see very well. There was a sort of drizzle that prevented us from seeing clearly, and a mist, too, that came from the volcano, a vapour that smelled of kitchen stenches and sewers.

"We didn't need to speak to one another. Each of us knew what the other was thinking about. Each of us said to himself, there, that's it, it's beginning again, so it will never ever end. And we continued walking. We drew closer to the shapes. We saw that, alas, we had not been mistaken, that once again these were drowned people, young black men, who looked as though they were brothers of the original three drowned men, who were just as young as them, just as dead as them, just as peaceful in their death.

"We dragged them to the shore. What was it we had done to deserve this? Or what had we not done? We began to weep. I had never seen you weep. And I no longer remembered that I could weep myself. When we had finished laying them out on the shingle, and we had looked out to sea, we saw through our tears that streams of other corpses were emerging, and that some of them were already washing up at our feet. Then we began again, we pulled them up onto the shore. We laid them out alongside the others.

"And the sea still brought in other drowned people. There was no end to it. We were exhausted. We were still weeping. Our arms and our backs hurt. We were breathless. We weren't the only ones. Without our realising it, all the inhabitants of the island had gradually appeared and all of them were dragging corpses, and all of them were weeping just as we were weeping. At every moment the sea was steering towards our feet dozens of corpses that were of an age at which it should be forbidden to die, and they all had the same solemn expression on their faces, one that entered our souls and asked that we be held accountable.

"The hours passed. It was not morning. It was not evening. There was no longer any night. There were only these drowned bodies which the sea never stopped setting down in front of us all, you, me and all the others on the island, and we dragged them onto the beach until eventually we could no longer see a single pebble; the beach had become a vast open-air cemetery, a cold chapel of rest, and there we all were, the inhabitants of the island, of this island which is the only one of all the islands in the Dog Archipelago to be inhabited, inhabited by wretched, ridiculous, old, selfish men, lost and in tears."

The Mayor had listened to the Doctor without interruption. There was a long silence. He raised his coffee cup to his lips and drank from it, wincing slightly, while continuing to look him in the eye. The sound of the clock behind him seemed to have grown louder. This gave him a headache. He continued to gaze at the Doctor, and he began to shake his head slightly, as one does in the presence of someone you feel sorry for because it distresses you to realise that he is not quite in his right mind.

"But my dear fellow," the Mayor eventually murmured to the Doctor, who was waiting anxiously for him to say something, "why do you call it a dream?"

THE END

PHILIPPE CLAUDEL is a university lecturer, novelist, film director and scriptwriter. He has written fourteen novels that have been translated into several languages. In 2009 his film "I've Loved You So Long", which draws upon Claudel's eleven years teaching in prisons, won the BAFTA Award for Best Film Not in the English Language. Among his novels, *Grey Souls* won the Prix Renaudot in France, the American Gumshoe Award and the Swedish Martin Beck Award. *Brodeck's Report* won the *Independent* Foreign Fiction Award in 2010.

EUAN CAMERON is a literary translator from the French and a former publisher. His previous translations include works by Patrick Modiano, Didier Decoin and Paul Morand, as well as biographies of Marcel Proust and Irène Némirovsky. His debut novel, *Madeleine*, was published in 2019.